THE THRUMMING STONE

Written by Brhel & Sullivan
Illustrated by Ryan Sheffield

CEMETERY GATES
MEDIA

The Thrumming Stone
Published by Cemetery Gates Media
Binghamton, New York

ISBN: 9781093989175

For more information about this book and other Cemetery Gates Media publications, visit us at:

cemeterygatesmedia.com
facebook.com/cemeterygatesmedia
twitter.com/cemeterygatesm
instagram.com/cemeterygatesm

Cover and interior illustrations by Ryan Sheffield
Cover layout by Burt Myers

CONTENTS

CANTICLE ONE

Even by lax cultural standards of the 1990s, my sister and I were probably too old to be rocketing down the hill at Virginia Ave Park. Jenny was 16 and I had just turned 14, but an impromptu afternoon of sledding freshly fallen snow was one of the last bastions of pure, unadulterated joy in our increasingly complicated lives. We were in the 8th and 10th grade at Lestershire High, coming of age during the peak of MTV's generational influence—thankfully, we were still a couple years away from voluntarily tethering our social lives to AOL and its Instant Messenger. And even though we were glued to MTV and reruns of *90210*, our worldview was still largely shaped by our family, friends, teachers, and small town.

Our passage into adolescence had been a rocky one. Our mother, Helen, had only been gone for a couple years, but her eulogy and burial still felt recent. Jenny and I were young enough that her absence was omnipresent in our daily lives—an empty seat at recitals, a dearth of home-cooked meals, missed rides to and from sporting events. Yet, there were moments between the two of us, here and there, which recalled the blissful innocence and wide-eyed optimism that had defined our childhood. We could still enjoy the holidays and looked forward to seeing our extended family; there were birthday parties, presents we hoped to receive, sleepovers and dances that we planned for months in advance.

Our idyllic, storybook village had not yet been laid to waste by layoffs and plant closings. Main Street still felt like the center of town. Everyone I knew had been at the Christmas parade, only weeks prior. It seems alien now, but there were two roller skating rinks, at which I had recently attended birthday parties; and this was the same year that I had started high school.

I was a nostalgic kid. Always looking to recreate monumental moments from my past, even though I was still just that—a kid who'd only just found his postpubescent voice. I was taken aback when Jenny brought up sledding. We only lived a few streets away from the best sledding hill in the county, and it had been such a centerpiece of our childhood winters.

We'd dug out my dad's old wood runner sleigh and a beat plastic sled that most people would have tossed after a season. A layer of fresh, powder snow had fallen that late-December morning, just right for speedy trips down the slick slope. The hill at Virginia Ave was already a canvas of intersecting lines and boot prints, but the park was largely empty when we got there. There were a few stragglers who were trying to erect a small snow ramp, but it kept flattening each time they hit it. We watched them while we made a few runs of our own, until they finally gave up and went home, and the park was ours.

"Maybe we should try down there," said Jenny, pointing to a smaller slope at the northern end of the park, running alongside one of the softball fields.

I just shook my head and laughed. Jenny always had to take an innocent outing and find a way to make it a little more dangerous, or at least involve some sort of trespassing. I had gotten scraped up by too many ledges, dogs, and thorn bushes to follow her blindly into another misadventure.

"Why not?" asked Jenny.

"It just goes down to the crick."

"C'mon, dude. I bet it's steeper."

"What if we hit the ice and fall in?"

Jenny snickered. "It's frozen over and the water's probably only ankle-deep, anyway." She began toward the other hill, dragging our dad's antique sled behind her, ignoring my warning. She didn't even look back to see if I'd follow. "If you fall in, I'll call Captain Kirk and you can be on *Rescue 911*."

I can't lie and say I didn't hesitate, but ultimately, by age 14 I had largely grown tired of playing the wimpy younger brother—especially since I now towered over her. I picked up my crappy, red sled and jogged to catch up.

This second hill was mostly forested, but there was a broad path that led from the edge of the softball field to the bank of the frosted-over creek—it certainly looked like it would be a fun, fast ride.

"There's no way that you won't go onto the ice, Jenny."

"There's nothing to worry about," she said. "I'm practically an Olympic-caliber sledder. I'll just turn before I hit the ice."

"Just be careful, okay?"

"Sure."

She set the sleigh at the edge of the hill and took a seat. But instead of pushing off down the steep embankment, she hesitated and looked back at me like she had been struck with a brilliant idea.

"You get on the back," she said. "More weight is better with these old sleds."

"No. You do it first."

"Don't be a wuss, Joey."

I sighed and got on the back of the sled. I knew she'd torment me for days if I didn't comply. She was great at telling everyone we knew about how much of a little bitch I was. I took some comfort in the fact that if we crashed, I'd likely land on top of her.

Jenny grabbed the rope and placed her feet on the steering board. "Ready?"

"No." I just assumed that with her at the helm things wouldn't end well.

"3....2....1!"

We shot off from our position and down the unmarred path. As we glided down the hill, we carved out two deep tracks in the snow; it really is amazing how fast runner sleighs can go. The sled picked up speed as we made our quick descent, and Jenny screeched with glee. Despite my initial trepidation, I couldn't help but crack a smile.

The slight bumps on the way gave us brief rushes of weightlessness, and a large stone or root sent us airborne. We only got a few inches off the ground, but tufts of snow shot up in our faces when we landed, and Jenny had to redirect us away from the trees that lined the left side of the path.

I knew that we were traveling too fast for her to steer us hard in any direction, and I think she recognized it soon after—though I now suspect that it had always been her intention to take us onto the ice. But she made no move to halt or alter our progress as we passed over the creek, the runners hissing beneath us as we traversed the ice. I suspect we even picked up speed over the twenty-or-so-yard-width of Little Choconut Creek, because we were propelled into the woods on the other side, narrowly avoiding a few gnarled maples and elms before slowing among a field of glacial erratics.

Jenny fell back against me and we rolled off the sled as it came to a halt. I yelped as I landed elbow to rock. "Get off!"

She sat up gingerly and shook some snow from her scarf. "Holy crap. That was—"

We were both startled by a loud groaning and then a series of *pops* from the ice behind us.

"See, I told you we wouldn't break through the ice," said Jenny, grinning. We got up and took a few steps back toward the creek to have a look at the source of the noise.

Our sled had evidently cut a section of the ice like a knife, because there was now a large gap which exposed the running water below.

"*C'mon!* How are we supposed to get back across now?" I instantly regretted not having the guts to just tell her no.

"Relax. We're still in Lestershire, bro. We'll just head this way until we get to Airport Road," said Jenny, pointing toward the rocky clearing where the sled had come to a stop.

"Yeah, I guess," I said. "I think I can hear a truck nearby."

We wandered the forest, trying to determine the direction of what sounded like an idling engine. We had never been in that part of the park before and, though I knew our house was still only a ten-minute walk, it suddenly felt like we were miles from civilization, shut off from the world. It was exhilarating—that adolescent call to adventure and exploration—we didn't get out of Lestershire all that often.

"Some of these rocks are pretty cool," I said. The landscape was unique, like something you'd find in the Catskills or Adirondacks, not smack in the middle of our little village. "I've never seen anything like this around here."

"I think it's this way," said Jenny, ignoring my comment. She started up a steep incline.

"Wait, Jenny, check this out," I said, approaching one of the larger stones in the field. It was between four and five feet tall but wasn't as round as the others; it reminded me of one of the smaller monoliths I'd seen in books about Stonehenge and other megalithic sites—I'd been obsessed with Stonehenge since elementary school. When I got closer to the stone, I first assumed that it was covered in faded graffiti but was pleasantly surprised to find out that the lines were carved into the rock.

"What?" She came back down but took her time in doing so.

"It looks like pictures, but like it's some sort of writing..."

"On the boulder?"

I looked at the squiggles and characters from different angles, tried to make some sense out of them. There were animals, people in conflict, indiscernible swirls that seemed to say something that I couldn't quite grasp. "It's like hieroglyphics, I guess."

Jenny came up beside me and examined the markings. "Yeah, wow... They're not hieroglyphics, though. They're called petroglyphs."

"What's that mean?" I asked.

"It just means someone made inscriptions on the stones. Probably Iroquois."

"Where'd you hear that?" I asked.

"Mr. Verity," said Jenny, referring to one of our school's more eccentric teachers. He had been her history teacher and now he was mine.

We dusted off as much snow as we could around the rock to get a better look at the carvings.

"So, you think this is really old?" I asked, tracing some of the intentional lines with my finger.

When she didn't respond, I leaned over to see what was occupying her attention, and was spooked by her now-frozen, emotionless expression. "Jenny?"

But I didn't have time to wait for a response, as I began to feel a vibration through my gloves, emanating from the monolith itself. A sudden wave of nausea swept over me and I felt a sickening fear of losing consciousness—the sort of stimulation where in the midst of the experience, you come to the conclusion that 'this is what it's like to die.' My racing thoughts only subsided when my vision narrowed to the point where I blacked out. What I experienced then is still difficult to describe. Because, in essence, I merely collapsed next to a rock in a snowy forest. I knew it to be all the same symptoms of passing out. I'd fainted in junior high shop class, during a grisly discussion of bandsaw and drill accidents; I knew the feeling well. But this experience had one noticeable difference, in that, between my loss of consciousness and the cloudy recovery of my faculties, a window into some sort of special knowledge was briefly cracked open and then swiftly slammed shut.

I sat and stared at my black snow boots for some time after coming to, trying to recall the fleeting image. It was an identical loss to the times I'd awoken from a nightmare but had no recollection of the terror I'd just experienced. For some reason, I felt like my boot was the only tenuous connection I had to the vision. My boot. *A soldier's black boot.* Soldiers walking through the desert during the Gulf War, in their hot, heavy gas masks.

"Joey?" came my sister's voice, shakily.

I looked up, immediately losing my train of thought. She was sitting too—with this pale, dazed expression that I'd only seen on bite victims in vampire movies.

"I don't hear the humming anymore," she said. Neither did I.

We both silently got up and headed up the incline, eventually finding our way through the woods and reaching the street that joined Airport Road and Virginia Ave. We didn't speak of our encounter with the vibrating, thrumming stone on our walk home either. I could tell that she was drained, though I didn't dare mention my vision, or ask her whether she had experienced anything uncanny at the monolith.

I think we both understood that the other had undergone some sort of trauma, and that the best course of action was to just leave it be.

CANTICLE TWO

I was a kid with a rich imagination. I was certain that my recurring dream where a UFO hovered over the turnaround near my friend Andy Kulowski's house had been a premonition, a gifted vision of things to come. That I had even predicted my Mom's departure from her body the same day I saw this bald man in all black walking the tracks on Lester Ave. Death on his mission to relieve her at Memorial Hospital from her withering, soul-crushing suffering.

So, when I began waking up in cold sweats, night after night, from nightmares of which I couldn't remember any of the details—I frustratingly knew that there was some vital information being transmitted to me, and that it stemmed from my encounter with the thrumming stone; I was certain of it. I just had to decipher it.

I had always felt an overwhelming glee during winter break—all the free time I had to play Nintendo and watch TV, for however long I wanted—but this year was different. I was on edge and even dreading another run-through of the nightmare that I couldn't quite grasp the meaning of. I hadn't spoken to Jenny about our experience at the park. I assumed she'd seen what I'd seen, but I hadn't had the courage to broach the topic with her. I figured that if asked her whether black boots and Desert Storm meant anything to her, she'd probably slug me.

It was one of the last days of our vacation and we were both excited for our friends to be staying overnight. My dad, Tim, had become a softie—a pushover, even—in the years following my mom's passing. He usually worked nights at the chemical plant (E. Johnson Chemical Corp.), so he probably figured he wouldn't really have to deal with us, and that we were old enough to babysit ourselves.

Lauren and Jason were another brother/sister tandem, the same grades as us. Their mother had babysat us in elementary school, and they only lived one street over, on Albany. They arrived and we ate pizza with my dad before his shift at the plant.

"I can't believe you kids are in high school already," said Tim, shaking his head. "It seems like just yesterday I was driving you guys to birthday parties at Chuck E. Cheese."

Jason's eyes lit up at the mention of our favorite childhood haunt. "Oh, man. Chuck E. Cheese. Remember when we beat *The Simpsons Arcade Game*?"

"Dude, that was the best," I said. "We must have spent like $100 in tokens."

"You mean *I* must have spent like $100 in tokens," said Tim.

I laughed. "Oh, yeah. Thanks, Dad."

"Yeah, thanks, Tim," said Jason. Dad preferred that our friends called him Tim.

"No problem. Those were good times. I know my wife enjoyed taking you guys there too."

"Mrs. Sullivan was such a cool lady," said Lauren. No one never called my mother by her first name, dead or alive.

Jenny revealed a half-smile, but I could tell she was uncomfortable with the conversation turning into a bittersweet reminiscence of Mom.

I changed the subject. "Dad, I bet you liked going because they let you drink beer."

"Well," he said, "for most adults, alcohol is more entertaining than *Pole Position*." Dad drank a little back then, but he'd really upped his intake after Mom passed.

"I can't believe they let you drink beer where kids are swimming through a ball pit and playing arcade games," said Jenny. "It's no wonder they closed it down."

"Yeah, and put in that dumb country-western bar," added Lauren.

"Well, A Dash of Dallas is better than some empty, boarded-up building," said Tim. "A lot of the guys from the plant go there and have a good time. Personally, I'd listen to that crap that they call rap before you'd catch me line-dancing." E. Johnson Chemical Corp, since Lester Shoe & Boot had gone bankrupt, was the number-one employer in Lestershire. We didn't know what my dad did exactly—his name tag read LEVEL 2 PRODUCTION MANAGER—I learned later that he was a maintenance engineer and was responsible for ensuring that the plant ran efficiently.

"When do you start at the nuclear power plant?" I asked. Petrosky Power Station was located just a few miles south of Lestershire, on the opposite side of the Susquehanna River. My dad had been grumbling for months about having to run teams at both the chemical plant and nuke plant. The state had contracted dozens of E. Johnson employees to help with a massive update to the power station.

"We start preliminary work at Petrosky Power tonight, actually," said Tim.

"Are you gonna run the reactor, like Homer Simpson?" asked Jason. Lauren rolled her eyes.

"No, my job's much more boring than that; but I'm sure we'll be eating plenty of donuts," said Tim. He looked at his watch. "Oh, boy—I gotta get going, gang. My shift starts at 7." He got up from the table and took his plate to the sink.

"Don't fall into a vat of chemicals tonight, Dad," said Jenny.

It was a stale joke, but still got a few laughs.

"Yeah, yeah. I won't turn into the Joker or Two-Face *or* a Ninja Turtle..." He grabbed his coat and waved goodbye as he slipped out the back door.

We spent the next few hours with Lauren and Jason, watching *Clarissa Explains It All* and eating junk food—but I was too distracted to enjoy my time with my friends. I couldn't stop thinking about the fleeting visions I'd had at the monolith, and my anxiety was clouding my ability to reason. At the time, I wouldn't have considered the possibility that I was grasping for meaning where there might be none, because an abnormal event *had* taken place—we were knocked unconscious by it.

I knew that I had to share my experience with someone. Jason was my oldest friend and closest confidant. I couldn't just come out and tell him about my vision, as it didn't even make all that much sense to me. I'd need to show him the stone, the inscriptions. See if he could detect the hum, the vibrations.

Eventually, my sister took Lauren upstairs and Jason and I drifted off to my room. My friend lay beneath the soft glow of the nightlight, tucked into my faded Ninja Turtles sleeping bag, and we chatted, mostly about video games and girls. When I'd gathered up the courage, I told him about the odd stone in the woods. Just enough that he might want to go and see it for himself.

"I think you're messing with me, Joe," said Jason, before yawning. "Indian carvings?"

"I swear on my mother, Jay."

I vividly remember how wide his eyes had grown then. He knew I was dead serious. "Alright. It sounds cool. Tomorrow we'll go and check it out."

#

Jason and I got up early the next morning to see the stone. We devoured Frosted Flakes and a pack of S'mores Pop-Tarts before donning our snow gear. I knew that my dad wouldn't be up for hours, and he wouldn't really care where we went anyway, so long as it wasn't near the abandoned factories across the railroad tracks.

"Remember that summer we found that box of *Playboys* in the turnaround?" asked Jason, as we walked beneath frosted pines and spruces, just east of Virginia Ave.

"Yeah. And I remember how pissed my mom was when she found that Jenny McCarthy issue in my dresser. She made me go to Mass every morning for a week."

"That was a great issue, dude," Jason snickered. "Totally worth it."

"She was fuming..." I couldn't help but laugh at the thought of my Catholic mom embroiled in a moral panic over the fact that her son wanted to see a nude woman.

"My mom wasn't as mad as yours. I just had to hang around Lauren for a few days," replied Jason. "We probably just watched *The Baby-Sitters Club* and *Dirty Dancing* a dozen times."

It was strange. I didn't miss my mom's overbearing presence—that steady hand determined to mold me

19

into something specific—but I kind of missed having someone invested in the goings-on of my daily life. I don't know whether it's the nature of most fathers, but my dad's guiding principle of parenting seemed to be more reactionary than interventionist. We were free to make bad decisions, then he'd be there to help us settle the wreckage.

I pulled the top of my coat around my neck as a brisk, bitter wind passed. It was cold out. Well below freezing. I became preoccupied by how flat the snowflakes fell from the sky. It was like they were too heavy to flitter. I was so distracted I stumbled on a tree root.

"You do know where we're going, right?"

"It's just down this embankment here." I led Jason to the rocky clearing, which was partially covered in freshly fallen snow. Seeing it again made me tense. I wasn't sure whether I could hear the humming yet.

"Do you hear anything?" I asked, nervously.

"No."

We approached the large erratic together. It was practically at the center of the clearing, though the arrangement of the smaller stones nearby seemed random; natural even.

"This is it?" asked Jason. "I thought it was gonna be bigger, like the black monolith in *Space Odyssey*."

"Yeah, it's not that big; but you have to see the markings."

I brushed the snow from the stone, revealing the petroglyphs. I could tell Jason was intrigued, maybe even unnerved.

"This is cool..." said Jason, as he inspected the stone. "What do you think it's trying to say?"

"I don't know."

Jason ran his finger through the carvings, tracing the curves and indecipherable symbols. We'd found a bunch of interesting stuff on our adventures over the years—old military ammunition cans with rusted cartridges, a mummified cat in a trailer—but the monolith was natural, and more mysterious for that fact.

"Maybe it's a tomb marker and this is an ancient curse," said Jason. "Like we read it out loud and it awakens a vampire or something."

"I somehow doubt that..."

"Look at these big boys over here," said Jason, pointing out a few characters. "It looks like they're giants or something. The little dudes with the spears are fighting them off."

I'd seen the battle before. I'd retained most of the petroglyphs from my first experience with the stone.

"Crap. I meant to bring a pencil and some loose-leaf, to trace some of this stuff."

Jason didn't appear to have any sort of physical reaction to the stone, so I prompted him to take off his glove and press his naked flesh to it. I was anxious—my own palms sweaty—as he quietly acquiesced and placed his hand on the rock.

"Nah, it doesn't feel like it's vibrating or anything, dude," said Jason.

"Yeah, I don't hear the humming either," I said. "Maybe things aren't right today..."

I didn't get to finish my thought—and it was the briefest of moments—but I recognized that Jason seemed to be someplace else entirely. And before I could process that he might be having a hallucinatory episode, he'd already snatched his hand away from the stone, cradling it as if he had been stung.

"What the hell was that?!"

"What did you see?"

"Huh?"

"What did you *see*?!" I yelled, grasping him by the shoulder.

"Humming," he said. "I hear the humming."

I was worked up, but I tried to calm myself to listen. "I don't hear it."

"It's coming from the rock, Joey..."

I watched in disbelief as Jason reached for the rock again. I nearly tackled him, but something gave me pause. I could now feel the rock vibrating through the air, thrumming around me—if not more vigorously than it had before. Time seemed to slow around me, but not to me, as my breathing and heart rate sped up. It felt like an eternity watching him reach for the monolith, make contact, then ragdoll to the snowy ground beside it.

"Jay?!" I yelled, as I fell to his side, grasping him.

Moments later, he came to with the same expression—the same pale, dumbstruck look that I'd seen on my sister.

"You saw it, didn't you?!"

He stared up at me, still dazed. "The valley burning?"

"No! The soldiers with gas masks."

He blinked a few times, as if he were clearing the visions from his head.

"No, don't do that!" I said. "You have to remember them!"

Jason sat up and pushed me off him. "Relax, dude."

"You didn't see any soldiers?" I asked, frantically.

"It wasn't like seeing *one* thing," he said. "That's why it's so confusing..."

"You said the valley was burning—which valley?"

"I don't know," said Jason, slowly getting to his feet, brushing away the snow. "It could be any valley, any town, really."

I didn't say anything. He seemed upset, and I figured that at least some of it had to have been directed at me for taking him out there.

"Let's get out of here, I guess," I mumbled.

We followed our footprints back through the forest and said very little to each other. I regretted taking him out there. It was selfish of me, knowing that I'd had nightmares myself after my first brush with the stone.

"It's so strange. I really don't remember any of the details now," he said. "Just that it made me feel super upset. Like when I saw my cat Zinger III get run over when I was a kid."

"I'm sorry, Jay," I said. "I thought maybe you'd have the same vision that I had, and you'd be able to help me remember stuff about it. But it sounds like what you saw was different..."

"And what the hell are you two doing out in the woods?" It was Jenny. She and Lauren had only just entered the forest from the road.

Jason and I were surprised. I think I garbled out something about porn mags.

"Smoking reefer. We got the madness," said Jason, smirking at the girls.

I was surprised at my friend's sudden, and welcome, change of tone.

"You took him to touch the rock?" said Jenny. It was more of an accusation than a question. You couldn't get anything past her.

"I wanted to show him the petroglyphs and stuff," I said.

"But he didn't *touch* it, right?" she asked.

"It's just a rock with some grade school art," said Jason. "Probably not authentic Iroquois stuff, anyway."

"What, you're an expert on rock carvings now?" asked Lauren, chuckling.

"I wouldn't go down there, Lauren," I said.

"Wait... So, everyone here has touched this weird rock except for me?" Lauren and my sister merely pushed past us on the trail.

"Lauren, it's really screwed up," said Jason, his true state of mind now unmasked. "I swear, it'll give you nightmares."

They didn't reply, but each stuck a finger in the sky to let us know that they had thoughtfully considered our warnings. I really didn't get my sister. She knew what it felt like; why would she subject her best friend to that feeling? I had a reason for doing it; I was doing research. I knew that she and Lauren were likely only out there for the thrill of it.

Jason and I followed the girls at a distance, morbidly curious what was going to happen if Lauren too encountered the thrumming stone. I was hoping that maybe Jenny had forgotten the way there, but I knew that our boot tracks would lead them right to the spot.

We waited in the forest above the clearing as the girls talked, gesturing toward the stone monument every so often. Lauren was just as absorbed as we had been in seeing all the different carvings on the rock.

"She's scared," said Jason. "She won't touch it. She wouldn't even watch an episode of *Tales from the Crypt* with me when we were kids. She's too chickenshit."

For whatever reason—maybe Jenny pressed her, or maybe the stone was doing its humming and vibrating thing, beckoning her curiosity—Lauren lifted her hand to the monolith.

"Lauren, wait!" shouted Jason. He sprinted down the embankment, toward the girls. I followed.

"What the hell?!" said Jenny, turning to see us stumbling down the hill. "Why are you two clowns following us?!"

"The stone is tapping into electrical energy or something. There might be bare power lines underground. We don't want you to get electrocuted, Lauren," I said, now huffing from my exertion. I was just making up stuff now, thinking that maybe we could scare her away.

"How come everyone else can touch it?" asked Lauren, looking around at each of us. "And most rocks are perfect insulators, genius."

Jason shook his head. "Remember that time when we were selling candy for school and we thought we saw a masked man hanging in that garage on Wren Street?"

Lauren nodded. "Yeah..."

"Well, remember when you had night terrors for a week because of it?" said Jason. "This stone is like some sort of nightmare machine."

"But if you touch it, you won't just have bad dreams—you'll *feel* like scary stuff is *happening* to you even when you're awake," I added.

Lauren rolled her eyes. "Sure, guys."

"The carvings on it are cool. Just don't touch it. Promise?" said Jason.

"Fine. I'll just look. It's probably got bird crap all over it, anyway."

The four of us stood silently at different points around the stone, while Lauren studied the petroglyphs up close. The air was still charged with fear, anticipation, and a palpable anxiety over whether someone would feel, hear, or see something strange. It didn't sit right. I'd never been to Stonehenge but had always heard that places like that had this twofold vibe about them. That they held an unfathomable depth of knowledge just below the surface (which we'd never quite tap into) but that they were also a locus of pain, sacrifice, and even death. This clearing within the woods near my boyhood home felt just like that.

Lauren was just inches away from the stone, admiring its etched symbols. I was so caught up in her first observation of the stone that I hadn't immediately detected the steady hum that had built up within my left eardrum. I turned my ear away from the monolith, and as soon as I did, I was overtaken by that now-familiar thrumming sensation. It felt like it emanated from *within my bones*, as opposed to passing to me from the stone. And I wasn't the only one affected. I looked to Jenny, then Jason, then Lauren, and I could tell without anyone saying so that they, too, felt the same rhythmic vibration.

"No, Lauren!" yelled Jason. But it was too late. Time made no sense in those moments. I *had* been looking at Lauren when her brother had shouted her name. But by the time I had reacted to Jason's warning and my eyes had focused on Lauren, she had already dropped her glove and was touching the cold, carved surface of the stone.

Jason lunged to break the fall of her thin, crumpling body only a beat later. I saw her head bounce off the monolith on the way down. The two of them piled up like dead wood against the rock. Jenny and I then dragged the pair away from that terrible monument, as if we were pulling our friends from a raging fire.

"Lauren! *Lauren?!*" Jenny shouted in her best friend's face, but Lauren lay still.

Jason was only momentarily catatonic. He came to and tears began streaming down his cheeks as he watched my sister attempt to wake Lauren.

Jenny knelt in the snow and cradled her best friend like a doll, placing her cheek to the girl's face. "She's still breathing." No one immediately said anything. We were all lost for a few tense moments.

"We've got to get her out of the forest," I finally offered.

I grasped Lauren under the legs, while Jenny and Jason lifted her torso. We were physically and emotionally drained, and it was a difficult trek back, but the three of us carried her limp body up the embankment and eventually out of the woods.

I didn't have any visions that day, nor did I glean any additional information about my prior experience in the clearing. But I now knew more of what that mysterious stone in the woods was capable of, and my dread—and fascination—only intensified.

CANTICLE THREE

While I might have avoided the physical source of my anxiety, the stone still loomed large in my psyche. The indescribable nightmares continued, and I awoke on my first day back to school no further along in deciphering those terrible images. I sat through my classes, not really interacting with anyone, faculty or classmates. The first day after winter break usually had an air of excitement about it—kids bragging about what they got for Christmas, reconnecting with friends who they hadn't seen or spoken to in weeks—but I was tuned out, entirely absorbed by the ecosystem of the stone and the four of us who had encountered it. It wasn't until the end of the day, when I had the opportunity to talk to Jason, Lauren, and Jenny on our walk home, that I felt any connection to those around me.

We met on the porch of Nandos, the pizza parlor next door to school, each grabbing a dollar slice, then began our 10-minute walk home. It was weird. We were usually cracking jokes and talking school gossip, but no one was really offering much. I broke the embargo.

"How are you feeling, Lauren?" I asked. She had regained consciousness on our walk back to the house. Everyone had shared their visions from the stone, and we'd really bonded over our experience. But we hadn't spoken as a group since.

"I'm okay," she said, meekly.

"That's good," I said. "I don't know what the hell it is or why it's in Lestershire, of all places, but I've been thinking—"

"Let's just shut up about it, Joe," interjected Jenny. "We're not going back. Let's just be done with it."

I didn't anticipate her being so sensitive about the stone. "Yeah, I understand what you mean, but that's not gonna stop Jason's nightmares or these crazy daydreams I have in the middle of algebra."

"*I haven't had any nightmares*," said Jenny, incredulous at the thought of it. "You don't go around school telling anyone about nightmare-inducing rocks in the woods behind Virginia Ave Park, alright?"

I knew it was more of a threat than a question seeking consensus.

"Yeah, Jenny, I already told everyone. Jaime Perot, Jaime Plew. All the popular Jaimes. It's a bigger deal than *My So-Called Life* getting cancelled."

"*Shut up!*" sneered Jenny.

"I don't think we should tell anyone either," said Lauren.

"We don't have to, but what if the nightmares don't stop?" I said.

No one said anything for a while as we continued home. Everyone busied themselves with their pizza slice.

We walked a few blocks before Jason spoke up. "I've been having this same dream every night," he said, without a hint of his usual sarcasm. "It's not what I saw at the stone, though. It's like I'm all geared up like a firefighter in the middle of one of those big wildfires they have out west, and I'm just surrounded by smoke and this circle of fire is closing in on me."

"I see stuff, too," said Lauren, emboldened by her brother's admission.

"Oh, c'mon," said Jenny. "Are you guys serious? What do you 'see' Lauren?"

"I think I see...dead people slumped over in cars, sometimes," said Lauren, struggling to get the words out. "I was looking out the window in Spanish class today, and for a moment I swear there were bodies piled up in the street."

"Gross," said Jenny. "Did my brother put you up to this?"

Lauren shook her head, then quickly looked away to avoid making eye contact with my sister.

"You haven't been having nightmares, Jenny?" I asked. It didn't make any sense. She had touched the stone the same as me, at the same time...

"Everyone has nightmares," said Jenny. "I don't remember any *good* dreams, either."

"So, you didn't see anything when you touched the stone?"

"Sure, maybe," said Jenny. "But I don't really remember much about it. You guys are making a bigger deal of it than..."

Just then a Cadillac went over the curb and onto the sidewalk, not ten yards in front of us. We froze, grasping each other as the elderly man backed off the sidewalk and, like nothing had happened, continued down Memorial Drive.

We didn't say much to each other the rest of the walk home. When it was time to split up in Pete's parking lot and go our separate ways, Jenny reiterated that we shouldn't tell anyone about the monolith in the woods. We all agreed; though my promise was half-hearted. I don't know who I would've told at the time, anyway. I couldn't imagine an adult would take our visions or nightmares seriously, and the only kids I trusted already knew about it.

#

The next time we saw Jason, he was slumped over on a bench outside Pete's Market, our morning meetup spot. His face was all red and swollen, and Lauren was sitting next to him, teary-eyed.

"What the heck happened to you?" I said. He really looked like hell.

"The Groome twins, man," he groaned." I cringed at their very mention. Lestershire's resident twin assholes. We had run into them a few times on our walk to school, and every encounter was unwelcome. They hated everyone in Lestershire who wasn't a dirty, red-headed Groome.

"They jumped you?" Jenny asked.

"Lauren was listening to her Discman and they came up and started bothering her and tried to yank it out of her hands. I told them to fuck off...and then this happened," he said, pointing to the swollen tissue beneath his right eye.

"I'm sorry I couldn't help, Jason," said Lauren.

"It's not your fault."

"Those guys are such assholes," said Jenny.

"Dude, you don't look good," I said. "I'll take you back home. Jenny, you and Lauren go on ahead."

The girls left and I walked Jason back to his house so he could get cleaned up. I didn't care about getting another tardy; detention was a joke.

"Okay, how are we going to get these fuckers back?" I said.

We threw out a few ideas—ambush them with paintball guns, offer them Mountain Dew bottles full of piss—but nothing felt worthy of the crime.

32

"Hold up," said Jason, his voice somewhat strained. A smirk formed over his bruised and busted lips. "I just thought of something..."

#

The following Saturday, Jason and I were back at Virginia Ave Park, only this time we were accompanied by identical twins Tom and Don Groome. They had come with us under the pretense that we would lead them to a box of nudie mags, but we had something much more memorable to show them.

"So, you guys come out here to beat off onto trees and rocks?" said Don. "Don't you freeze your peckers off?"

"They probably bust into the snow, to hide the evidence," added Tom. He and Don laughed; we didn't.

"Nah, we just hide 'em out here," I said. "It's easier getting caught with one instead of a stack of 'em."

"Sounds like Sullivan's still getting whupped by his daddy," said Don.

"You're gonna have to stand up to your old man," said Tom. "We've been undefeated since puberty."

Somehow, I doubted that. Mr. Groome was one of the largest specimens of man that I'd ever encountered.

"He's gotta get through puberty first," said Don, smirking at his brother.

"It's right down here in this clearing," said Jason. We were both too driven by our mission to let their snide comments get to us. "See that big rock in the middle? We hide our crate at the base of it."

I hated being out there with them. It felt so isolated—even though we weren't all that far from roads and houses—the forest around us was dense and uninviting. There was always the threat that the twins would get bored and take their boredom out on us.

Plus, the thought of coming into physical contact with the stone again made my stomach uneasy.

We led them to the monolith. I could tell that Jason was uncomfortable being back there too, as he wouldn't really look at the stone directly.

"Where's the porn?" asked Tom, walking around the stone and inspecting its base.

"Hold up," I said. "Before we show you guys, you gotta prove you're not a couple of pussies."

I gulped when both boys turned to face me, as they were likely ready to answer my challenge with their fists.

"You sure you wanna do this, Sullivan?" asked Don.

I looked to Jason, unsure if I had the guts to continue with our plan.

"This is a witch's stone," said Jason, ending our momentary standoff. He went over to the rock in order to point out the petroglyphs. "One of the old Lester women from Sunshire Hill, from way back, practiced witchcraft out here, and these markings are her spells. She poisoned her maids while trying to raise Satan, and a mob eventually chased her down here and hung her from a tree—that one right over there." He pointed to a large pine with the darkest bark around.

"If you touch the rock for a couple minutes, the witch will call out to you," I ad-libbed.

"That's some major bullshit," said Tom.

"No, it's not," said Jason. "It really happened."

"It's true," I said. "We did it the other night."

Don grabbed Jason by the collar with both hands and pinned him against the monolith.

"Oof!"

"C'mon, guys..." I didn't get a chance to finish my thought, as Tom next tackled me and then pinned me to the ground.

"I want to see some titties," said Tom. *"You better not be fucking around."*

"There are no *Playboys* out here, guys. We just wanted to show you this creepy-looking rock," said Jason, ending the charade.

I turned my head in time to see Don punch him in the stomach. Jason crumpled to the ground, groaning and sucking air. Tom then pushed my head through the snow until I hit the hard, frozen dirt. I flailed my arms and legs, but Tom had a solid thirty pounds on me.

"Bring him over here," said Don.

I was terrified, unable to do much of anything, as Tom dragged me to my feet and then pushed me against the stone. With little fanfare, Don punched me in the gut, and I fell next to my friend.

"They need to learn to never fuck with us," said Tom. His brother agreed.

When I turned over, I saw that Don was bracing to either stomp or kick Jason, while Tom was leaning down to grab me. I shut my eyes and winced in anticipation of a punch or kick that never came. I then became acutely aware of my body growing numb to the cold that had previously surrounded me, while the sound of the wind rushing through the trees and the trickle of the nearby creek both dulled in my ears, as if an amplifier knob in my head was being turned toward zero.

A familiar humming then invaded my senses and the ground began to vibrate beneath me. I opened my eyes to see a moment frozen in time. Don with his left palm against the stone, one foot raised to hurt my friend, and Tom with his fingertips grazing the rock as he grasped my coat. It was like I could feel the rock and hear the humming by way of Tom as conduit. But I had no visions, while the brothers were clearly under the power of the thrumming stone—their eyes glazed over, their faces devoid of expression.

"Are you seeing this?" whispered Jason. His leg twitched beside me.

Don and Tom had begun to gently shake, as if they were now an extension of the stone. Their eyes rolled back in their heads, reminiscent of every possession ghost story I'd ever seen. A trickle of saliva seemed to be cresting Tom's bottom lip. I instinctively separated myself from Tom, but the grotesque scene continued to play out.

When Jason and I began scooting away, it seemed to cause some sort of break in the stone's grasp on the twins. Tom immediately face-planted in the snow, and moments later Don came tumbling after. However, the boys didn't move once they had fallen. Their bodies lay stiff, Don partly on top of Tom.

"Let's get out of here," I said.

We got up and began running, only slowing once we made it to the top of the embankment.

"They're still not moving," said Jason, as he paused to look back down into the clearing.

"They'll be fine," I said, shrugging off the possibility that they were worse off than we had been.

We kept going, abandoning Tom and Don in the snow.

The weekend passed and I didn't hear anything around the neighborhood about Tom or Don, so I assumed that they had found their way out of the woods. In hindsight, it was cruel to leave them unconscious in the dead of winter where no one would find them, no matter how terrible they had treated us.

I was relieved when I saw them at school that Monday; they looked fine, like their normal moronic selves. But then my next thought was that they were going to rough me and Jason up for tricking them. However, when the brothers saw me in passing that morning, they kept their distance.

"Did you happen to run into Tom or Don today?" I asked Jason that afternoon, as we walked home from school. Jenny and Lauren were a few yards behind us, gossiping about some heartthrob upperclassmen.

"Yeah," said Jason.

"Did they seem...off to you?"

Jason nodded. "It was a really weird day, Joe. It was almost like they were afraid of me..."

"They're probably having a bunch of nightmares. Maybe they think *we* did it to them, like we had some kind of control over it." I was nearly giddy at the thought of it.

"Like we're black mages or something?" said Jason.

The girls had sidled up to us. "What are you guys talking about?" asked Jenny.

I looked to Jason. We both knew that we had made a pact to not tell anyone about the stone. My sister was going to be pissed.

"We *might've* taken the Groome twins out to the stone to try and scare them. You know, to get them back for what they did to Jay and Lauren." I awaited my sister's disdain.

"It worked," added Jason.

"What stone?" asked Jenny.

I chuckled. "*What stone?* Funny."

"Really, Joey. What stone?"

"Oh, I don't know, the *freakin' magic humming monolith at Virginia Ave Park.*"

"Oh, yeah," said Jenny, looking briefly to Lauren to see if she was tracking. "The Freddy Krueger rock."

"Did they beat you guys up for showing them some dumb rock in the woods?" asked Lauren.

"What are you talking about, Lauren?" asked Jason. "That thing *knocked you out.* It's terrifying. Tom and Don practically crapped their pants."

"Actually, they might have," I added. "We didn't exactly check."

"Sure thing, guys," said Jenny. She and Lauren looked at each other and began laughing, then went on ahead to continue their gossip.

I couldn't believe it. I knew when Jenny was messing with me—she always did this weird thing with her nose—but she had been totally serious just then. She and Lauren hadn't exactly forgotten about the thrumming stone, but they had certainly under-estimated its power. But why?

Jason looked at me, shaking his head. "What's wrong with our sisters, dude?"

"It's like they're slowly forgetting about it," I whispered. "I don't get it."

"Maybe they've really stopped having the nightmares. Remember when Jenny denied having any?"

"What about Lauren?" I asked.

"She was in real bad shape only a week ago, dude," replied Jason. "Now it seems like it's not a big deal to her."

"It *has* been a while since I've had any nightmares, Jay..."

"I didn't want to jinx it—but I haven't had any nightmares or visions the last couple nights either," said Jason.

"Since we took the twins to the rock, right?"

Jason nodded. "It's like we passed it on..."

In a way, I was relieved that my friends were forgetting about the stone and were no longer having disturbing dreams. But I felt that our discovery had to be important in some way, and that whatever visions we had experienced really did matter. And I didn't want to forget any of it.

When I got home, I grabbed some paper and a charcoal pencil from my mom's makeshift art studio. Dad had said for years that he was going to pack it away; but the desk and easel continued to sit there, ready should her spirit ever return.

I sketched the visions that I recalled—and the nightmares of my friends—to the best of my ability. I drew as many of the petroglyphs as I could remember, then made journal entries about each of our encounters in the clearing, documenting every last detail. I hoped that if I really began to forget, I'd be able to use this record to jog my memory, and perhaps it might aid me in solving the puzzle of the monolith itself.

#

Mr. Verity was easily my favorite teacher, and his second-period history class was one of the only classes that I found genuinely engaging. Unlike most teachers at Lestershire High, he seemed excited to discuss the subject matter, and his enthusiasm was contagious—he somehow made even humdrum events like the

Opium Wars interesting. He had been an Army drill sergeant at one point, and no one dared bullshit or lie to him, but he was also one of the only teachers whom kids sought out beyond the confines of the classroom.

Mr. Verity stood in front of the blackboard. He wore a red tie and his white dress shirt fit a little too tight to his broad, fit frame. He sported a buzz cut, as if he might get called back to his platoon any day, but it was probably just a good way to conceal his receding hairline.

"How many of you are familiar with the Great Plague, the Black Death?" he asked. Practically every-one raised their hands.

"Now, how many of you have heard of the Spanish flu?" asked Mr. Verity. Dave Ovens, the biggest brown-nose in class, was the only one to raise his hand. "Well, the Spanish flu was one of the deadliest pandemics in human history. It affected approximately 500 million people, and killed as many as 100 million, spreading from the Arctic Circle to the Pacific islands. The world's population at the time wasn't even two billion. Just think about what would happen if there was a disease that impacted the lives of one in four people living today."

I was dumbfounded that I hadn't heard about the Spanish flu before. It seemed like such a monumental event, and it had happened within the lifetime of people I knew. My great-grandma had only recently passed, and she would've been a teenager in 1918.

When Mr. Verity paused, I raised my hand. "Yes, Joe?"

"Why isn't the flu a big deal anymore?"

"Vaccines. We have a better understanding of public health, preventative medicine, a variety of other factors," replied Mr. Verity. "But some experts think that we might be sleeping on the dangers of the flu. A pandemic level strain is always only a winter away…"

Dave Ovens, per usual, had to add his two cents. "Penicillin wasn't discovered until ten years after World War I."

"Dave, how do you think the Great War plays into all this?" asked Mr. Verity.

"Thirty to forty million people had just died from one of the bloodiest conflicts in human history. Another fifty or so million dying all over the globe from the Spanish flu over a harsh winter or two just isn't as good of a story."

"I think you're onto something, Dave," said Mr. Verity. "The traumas of war are largely how we've defined ourselves and our history since our inception as a nation. This year's syllabus is a good example. Soon we'll be talking about the Second World War, then the Cold War, and eventually the Vietnam War."

Mr. Verity soon concluded his discussion and assigned us a chapter to read from our textbook.

"Dude, the Spanish flu was worse than the Black Death," I said to Jason as we left class.

"I always thought 'Spanish flu' meant a girl who was really horny or something," he replied.

I couldn't help but chuckle. "You should probably keep that to yourself, buddy."

We went out to the hallway and passed a disheveled Don Groome, who avoided eye contact with us. Seeing him reminded me of the thrumming stone. I started to tell Jason about my drawings and the journal I was keeping regarding our encounters, but he didn't seem all that interested.

"Huh, a journal?" asked Jason as we weaved past our classmates.

"Yeah, so I don't forget…" I said, quietly.

"Forget what, dude?" He looked at me dumbly.

"Ha-ha. Okay, *Jenny*. Don't screw around. I think it's important that we keep track of everything."

"Yeah, right...the nightmare rock," said Jason, flatly. "Maybe we are supposed to forget about it..."

I didn't respond. It bothered me that he'd said it, but I wasn't going to make a scene in the hallway at school.

CANTICLE FOUR

To my surprise, Valentine's Day was a big deal at Lestershire High. Guys and girls sent and received carnations, which were delivered during afternoon periods, interrupting class, causing anticipatory excitement to swell throughout the school.

I sat beside a pretty redhead named Stephanie Hoyt in math class and watched her 'ooh' and 'ahh' over a freshman girl's bouquet. It was the first time in my life that I had ever considered doing something to impress a girl. Up until that afternoon, ideas of what I might do to let a girl know that I was interested were purely hypothetical. Thought experiments for some distant time when I was able to adequately communicate my thoughts and desires to an amorphous female peer.

"It's kind of cheesy, right?" I whispered to Stephanie.

She eyed me, then wrote a note in response, flipping it to me when Ms. Hall turned her back to address an algebraic equation on the blackboard.

The note read: *Girls like getting stuff like that! Don't laugh Joey. Also, I have a long question for you (which will take some time to explain.) Meet me at my locker after last period. Ok?*

I was able to catch the Key Club before they shut down their flower operation and paid them $5 to send

Stephanie a pink carnation for last-period French. The fact that I wouldn't be in the class to witness, or take immediate credit for, the flower certainly helped me push through the flush-faced embarrassment of making such an out-of-the-blue gesture.

I couldn't pay attention during Spanish. I was watching the clock, sweating through my thin rugby sweater. It was pure torture; and I had to race to make sure that I got to Stephanie's locker before her.

Jason happened to be passing by and stopped to chat. "Today was wild, right?"

"Valentine's Day stuff?"

He nodded. "What kind of dork sends flowers to a girl at school?"

"A real tool," I said, nervously looking down the busy hallway for Stephanie.

"You wanna come to my locker with me?" he asked.

"Nah, go on ahead, I'll catch up," I said.

"What'd you just have—gym?"

Was I really sweating that bad? "Give me a break, dude..."

He'd figured it out and didn't need to say a thing. He really was my best friend.

"I'm waiting for Stephanie Hoyt," I said. "I need to get some notes from her."

"Sure, pal. See ya!" Jason laughed then went on his way.

Moments later I heard Stephanie call out to me. "Yo, Joe!" When I turned, she playfully poked me in the face with the pink carnation.

"Hey!" I stared dumbly into those big, green eyes of hers. It didn't take long before I felt awkward about it and averted my gaze.

"Thanks for my flower. It's so sweet of you!" she said. "I hope you didn't think I was asking you to send me one in my note. I don't want you to think I'm like that."

"I wanted to," I said. I didn't know what else I was supposed to say, to get at whether she liked me.

She opened her locker and rummaged through her backpack. I cringed when I looked in her locker mirror and saw a bead of perspiration running down my flush red face. I think Stephanie caught sight of my spasm, because she wrinkled her nose at me in the mirror.

"Anyway, I was wondering if you'd go with me to Virginia Ave Park some day after school this week? I was thinking about doing some extra credit for Mr. Verity's class—I need to do something to get my average up—and since you seem to know a bunch about history, I thought you might want to work on the project with me."

I felt sick to my stomach as soon as Stephanie mentioned Virginia Ave. "What kind of project?"

"You might've already heard. But there's this stone with these ancient drawings in the woods, out behind the park."

"No, I haven't heard anything." A nearly in-capacitating dread wracked my body at the mention of that forbidden rock. I was astonished that Stephanie, of all people, had knowledge of it.

"Oh, good," Stephanie said, shutting her locker. She seemed almost giddy about it. "You'll think it's neat. There's this big rock out there and it has all these Native American carvings on it. I figure we just have to take some pictures of the rock, find an expert at the university to help us identify what tribe made it..."

"Wait, you've already been out there?" I was nauseous. I felt like I'd puke if she said she had.

"Yeah, kinda..."

"Who took you out there?" I demanded. I knew she could tell something wasn't right by my tone, because she took a step back and hesitated.

"Um...Tommy Groome," she said.

My heart sank into my gut. "Stephanie...who else knows about the stone?"

"I don't know," she said. Her enthusiastic expression had faded. "Listen, it's cool if you don't want to do the project..."

"You've been having nightmares, right?"

She looked at me then like I'd just caught her in a terrible lie. Like I'd read her mind and she was ashamed of what she'd been thinking. "Yeah, I guess. How'd you know?"

"What did you see?"

"I don't want to talk about it," said Stephanie. I could tell she was stressed out about it.

"Please, tell me if you know of anyone else who's gone out there."

"Tommy just said he and his brother found it," she replied. She paused to look around, as if someone else might be listening in on our conversation. "Nicole Baylor and I went out there with them. It was a real trip."

"What did you see, Stephanie—when you touched it?"

"It was so messed up," she said, again looking around to see if anyone was listening. "And I keep seeing it, but not only in my dreams. There's this old ship with giant sails coming down a river, and it's burning..."

Her bottom lip quivered when she'd trailed off.

"Please, tell me everything you can remember about it," I pleaded. I didn't want to upset her, but I needed to know what piece of the puzzle the rock had bestowed upon her.

"I gotta go, Joe..." she said abruptly, before jogging off and merging into the rush of kids headed for the exits. I nearly called after her, even took a few steps as if to follow—in case she had that last thread which could pull the tapestry of nightmares together. But I somehow managed to check myself, momentarily restrain my impulse toward discovery—she clearly didn't want to talk anymore about her visions—so, I went on my way.

Jason caught up with me at my locker a few minutes later. "How'd it go with Stephanie?"

"She knows, dude," I said.

"Knows that you're a dork?" He laughed.

"The Groome twins took her and another girl to the stone."

Jason was shocked. "*Huh?* Really?"

"She wanted me to go with her," I said. "She had no clue that I knew what it was."

"Crap. She was trying to get you to go touch it?"

I nodded. "And why do you think that is?"

Jason punched the locker next to mine. "I'm sorry, Joey. I think I really fucked up..."

"We both took the twins out there. It's both of our faults..."

He cut me off. "No, Don came to me a few weeks back—you know—not long after we figured out that we were forgetting about it."

"What'd you tell him, Jay?"

"He practically begged me, Joey. I felt bad, and they hadn't been messing with anyone at school. I thought that we might've really taught them a lesson..."

"And?"

"I just told Donnie how it went after you showed me, and how we stopped having nightmares after we took them out there."

"So, they took new people out to the rock to try and pass it on?" I asked.

Jason nodded slowly. "Sounds like it."

"Christ. What if this thing starts spreading through school like some sort of disease?"

"A nightmare plague," said Jason. "This might not end well."

"We gotta do something about it, dude. We gotta warn people, since we're the ones that started it."

"It's the kind of thing that you just have to let run its course. It'll become gossip, but it might not spread too far if we keep quiet about it," said Jason, half-heartedly.

"I don't know why, but since the beginning I've felt like it all means something, man. It's gotta be more than just a nightmare rock."

"I really don't want to deal with it anymore, Joey." The tension was there between us. I felt passionate about my position; we needed to do something.

"If we've unleashed some sort of nightmare plague on this school, we're obligated to at least try to do *something* about it, Jay."

"You started it, Joey," said Jason. "You and your sister pushed your nightmares off on me and Lauren."

I couldn't believe how cold he was being. We'd been best friends since kindergarten, gone through everything together growing up, the death of my mother even, and he'd never used that nasty of a tone with me.

"You act like I did it on purpose," I said.

"Joe, at this point I'm not sure what you meant to do."

"That's harsh, Jay."

We didn't walk home together that afternoon.

In a matter of weeks, the tenor of the student body at Lestershire High had dramatically changed. In burying our fears—and likely our responsibility—Jason and I had allowed a plague of nightmares, rumors, and traumas to spread throughout our school unchecked. I imagined Lestershire High as one of those massive cruise ships—a week away from the nearest port—with norovirus threatening to disable every passenger and crew member on board. By early March, I could no longer tell whether the number of kids that had encountered the thrumming stone was in the dozens or hundreds.

My classmates were absent, drinking heavily, some were even vomiting at school due to their visions. The irritability factor from loss of sleep was palpable— fistfights broke out in gym class over games of dodgeball, there were shoving matches in the cafeteria over seating arrangements—and no team of Dream Warriors was going to combat it. Our teachers and the administration were aware that their school was falling apart. They had countless meetings, even brought in a psychologist and drug-sniffing dogs to try and get a handle on the issue. The problem wasn't that they refused to recognize the symptoms—they didn't have the training to diagnose the disease. Pamphlets, drug abuse lectures, psychologists, and D.A.R.E. officers might have helped if the issues were drugs, STDs, mononucleosis, or grief over the death of Kurt Cobain—no one was trained to recognize a teenager afflicted by a paranormal seeing stone in the woods.

I kept my ears open for hushed talk of the visions, horrific dreams, who I knew for sure went back to the stone to tempt fate for a second or third time, and I wrote it all down. If any of it meant anything, I was going to have a record. I knew kids were starting to forget; some would go back simply because they remembered going, while they weren't sure if they had experienced anything of note on prior trips. Thankfully, most didn't seem to know that they could pass on their suffering to new recruits.

I really felt helpless at the time and didn't know who to tell. I knew my Mom would have at least heard me out. She had been the one to listen to me babble on about alien sightings in the turnaround, disappearing staircases in the woods, and bloodstained rocks in Valleyview Cemetery. I had never seriously considered telling my dad about anything out of the ordinary. He couldn't be bothered by nonsense kid stories, and his mind was always wrapped up in his work anyway. But I had to tell *someone,* and with limited access to adults who knew anything about local history and magic seeing stones, I decided that my best chance was with Mr. Verity.

"How many of you know what a fallout shelter is?" asked Mr. Verity.

I shot my hand up. I wanted to get his attention during class. Luckily, he called on me instead of Dave Ovens. "They're for people to hide out in during nuclear attacks."

"Correct," said Mr. Verity. "Fallout shelters were commonplace in the 1950s and 1960s, at the height of the Cold War. My father built an underground shelter near our home in Waverly. I was young at the time, but it made my family, and millions of Americans like us, feel a little safer during those troubling times."

"Was it true that kids used to get under their desks to protect themselves from nuclear attacks?" asked Dave Ovens.

"Yes, Dave. We'd get on our hands and knees under our desks during drills," said Mr. Verity. "For a period of time, a nuclear war with Russia seemed imminent."

Someone else asked about his family's fallout shelter, hoping to get him off on a tangent. Mr. Verity was prone to long, interesting digressions that had little to do with the scheduled coursework.

"I promise to tell you all about my father's bomb shelter once we're finished with the chapter that covers Chernobyl," said Mr. Verity. "It's actually still intact beneath Waverly Glen Park. Though it's sealed now, so I can't exactly give you a tour."

Everyone laughed.

"My dad says that nuclear power plants are a bigger threat than nuclear war," said Dave Ovens. Most of my classmates groaned.

"They might be, especially now that the Soviet Union has collapsed," said Mr. Verity. "But there are also tremendous benefits to nuclear power—not to mention, our local energy plant employs over a thousand people. I promise, we'll get to all this nuclear stuff when we get to the Chernobyl disaster."

After class, I approached Mr. Verity, unsure with how I might broach the subject of the thrumming stone. He was a level-headed guy, and I knew I couldn't just blabber on about visions and whatnot.

"Hey, Joey. What's going on?"

"Mr. V, do you have a few minutes?" I said. "I wanted to ask you about Native American history."

"Yeah, sure; I'm free. I'm no expert in the field but go ahead."

"Well, I don't know if you've heard, but we've found a stone in the woods with a bunch of Iroquois petroglyphs. That's what we're guessing, anyway. I've drawn some of them from memory, and I was wondering if you knew what they might mean."

I handed him a few of my loose-leaf drawings.

Mr. Verity looked over the pages with interest. "There's really a rock in the woods with these carvings?"

"Yeah, it's a big stone that my sister and I found over winter break," I said. "I don't know if kids are drinking out there now and putting graffiti on it, but I'd like to know what the pictures mean."

"A couple kids have mentioned this to me over the last few months, but no one ever brought me anything, or told me exactly where it was," said Mr. Verity. "Shoot. This could be authentic. Can I copy these and send them to a buddy of mine at the university?"

"Yeah, sure," I said. I was worried that he'd ask me where the monolith was. I really didn't want to find out what would happen if a bunch of adults started going out there and touching it. Lestershire might turn into some sort of nightmare town, like Haven in *The Tommyknockers*. "Doesn't it look like they're fighting giants?"

"Yes, could be. Iroquois and Susquehannock legend cover giants in New York, but so do Washington Irving and the architects of the Cardiff Giant hoax, for that matter," said Mr. Verity, grinning. I'd seen the Cardiff Giant at the Farmers' Museum in Cooperstown a few summers before.

"There's a boat with a sail here, so I wouldn't say these petroglyphs were more than a few hundred years old," said Mr. Verity, pointing to a ship near the scene of conflict. "Native Americans never developed sails. This very well could tell of the coming of the Dutch to New York."

I could tell he was getting excited at the prospect. I thought it was neat, as I'd never noticed the image of the ship before. "Too bad the Iroquois couldn't have foreseen the coming of the white man..." I stopped myself because I'd had an epiphany.

"Unfortunately, I don't know that it would have mattered if they'd had a crystal ball, Joey," said Mr. Verity. "It's believed that 90% of the native population on the continent was wiped out during a series of epidemics after first European contact."

"Thanks for your time, Mr. V.," I sputtered. "I don't want be late for my next class."

Mr. Verity called after me as I hurried from the room. "This could be a great discovery, Joey. Stop at the history office after school and I'll make some copies of your drawings!"

My thoughts were racing. Why wouldn't the thrumming stone have given people visions in the past? The Iroquois might not have made the mysterious stone, though they obviously knew its significance. What if the carvings were an artist's clairvoyant nightmares from hundreds of years ago? A warning of the coming of the Europeans? There weren't exactly images of people afflicted with smallpox, from what I could tell—but who knows what the differences were from my drawings and the actual rock, since I'd drawn them from memory. I was surprised that I'd sketched a boat with a sail and hadn't recognized it for what it was.

I was certain now, where I had only suspected before, that my traumatic visions, everyone's frag-mented nightmares, was a group premonition of something horrible to come. When I got home and pored over my now-copious notes, I knew that the event would occur locally. Kids had described familiar places, neighborhoods, and landmarks in their visions. With talk of nuclear disaster and fallout shelters fresh on my mind—paired with my personal visions of masked soldiers barricading avenues out of the

56

valley—I knew there could only be one source for such an apocalyptic event. Something bad was going to happen at the nuclear power plant across the Susquehanna River. Maybe there'd be a meltdown while they were upgrading it—some maintenance issue would go unnoticed, leading to disaster—and perhaps the monolith even chose me because my dad worked there!

While I didn't know how to proceed in warning people—what I could actually do to prevent the event—I knew enough that I could prep for disaster. I could educate myself, and I'd heard that the local Army & Navy surplus store owner was an avid doomsday prepper. Radiation was going to be the biggest issue. I could still shovel some more driveways to make money, mow lawns eventually, do chores around the house. Maybe no one would listen, but I could at least be ready, do something for myself and my family.

CANTICLE FIVE

"Dad, say there was a meltdown at the power plant—what would happen exactly?"

"We'd contain it quickly. There are too many safety precautions in place," Tim replied, putting down his newspaper. "Three Mile Island was an invaluable learning experience."

We were sitting in the living room with the evening news on; Jenny was out with her friends. The few hours that my dad wasn't at work or sleeping between shifts were precious to me, especially when it was just the two of us.

"Could it set the whole valley on fire?" I asked.

He raised his eyebrows at something Dan Rather said before looking at me. "It's been unseasonably warm for March, buddy. Why aren't you out riding bikes with Jason or playing ball?"

"Dad, I'm worried that there's gonna be a nuclear disaster and that it's going to be really bad." He was shaking his head and rolling his eyes before I'd even finished.

"Joe, I think it's great that you're reading science and engineering books, and yeah, it's odd that you're at the Army surplus store every weekend—but I haven't seen you with your friends in weeks."

I didn't understand why he always dodged questions about his work. I figured he'd be excited to talk shop with me. What father wouldn't want to have a son who was curious about his livelihood? "It's been a long winter. Baseball practice doesn't start for another couple weeks…"

"You're still young—it's not like I'm asking you why you don't have a girlfriend, or why you're not out drinking in the woods with your pals. Your grandpa used to ask me stuff like that, and it upset me. I've just noticed that you've become much more introverted over the last couple months."

"I've been having these bad dreams about there being a nuclear disaster in town," I said, flatly. "It's not as bad as it was, but a bunch of kids at school have been having similar nightmares…"

"Trust your dad. Nothing's gonna happen at the power plant. I've overseen everything that's gone on during the upgrade; and you know me, I'm detail-oriented to a fault," he said, before changing gears. "Do you think you should talk to a psychiatrist, Joey? We're coming up on that certain time of year…I'd go with you, if you want me to. I like talking about her."

I couldn't fault my dad for not listening. But it was monumentally depressing that what he heard—what he was selectively listening for—was buried grief over my mom. "Yeah, maybe you're right, Dad."

It wasn't long before he was grabbing his coat and keys to leave for his evening shift. "Hey, Dad, could you double-check the integrity of the steel containment vessels in the reactor for me?"

He grinned at my esoteric question. "Sure, pal. But it'll have to wait until Monday. I'm actually at E. J. Chemical tonight. I have a ton of work that I'm behind on up there."

"Thanks, Dad."

Saturday morning at Bernie's Army & Navy on Main Street always included a cast of characters. It was mostly war vets over fifty hanging around, while a few Boy Scouts would come through looking for camping gear and MREs, and then there was me. The vets would first congregate at the Red Robin Diner across the street, then they'd head over to Bernie's at eight o'clock with their steaming cups of coffee, where they'd kill time before the Legion hall opened.

My dad had frequented the Army & Navy as a teenager in the 1960s. When we'd pass by, he'd always remark that going into Bernie's was like stepping into a time warp—and the few times that we did go in together, he'd say that it had that same musty smell when he was a kid. Bernie and most of the guys knew my dad by name. Sure, he was a manager at the chemical plant, but he'd also been a star athlete in high school, and that got you lifelong notoriety in a small town like Lestershire.

I'd become a fixture at Bernie's for purely practical reasons. I had been slowly acquiring pieces for a MOPP suit (MOPP is the variety of military acronym that when broken down only creates more questions than answers. I'll just say that one of the 'P's stands for 'protective.') A MOPP suit can provide protection against radiation via its gas mask, hooded blouse, pants, overboots, and gloves. I, like most Americans, first caught sight of these suits during CNN's coverage of the Gulf War. The fear was that Saddam had chemical and biological weapons, and it was a sensible fear, because it turns out our government used its satellites to help the Iraqis launch chemical attacks against Iran in the 1980s.

"Brady Bill's certainly hurt my side business," said Bernie. He was behind the counter, holding court while five of his pals stood in a semicircle in the aisle. I couldn't really tell how old these guys were, but they all sort of looked the same: beer gut, white streaks running through their hair, fishnet military ball caps. All I really knew about them was that they'd fought in Vietnam, Korea, and World War II—because that's all they ever talked about. Twenty, forty, and even fifty years later they were still giving updates on these conflicts like they were recent events; so, I couldn't help but be curious about, and listen in on, their conversations.

"Clinton and his ilk aim to destroy the Second Amendment," said Bernie. "Imagine if those terrorists hadn't been absolute morons and had a sensible bomb under the World Trade Center? Clinton would've used it as an excuse to take away every last means of protection a man can have."

Bernie's audience grumbled in agreement to just about everything he said. My dad always said there were more guns in America than Americans, that it was a silly thought that the government would have the time to rummage through everyone's closets grabbing rifles and shotguns.

"Martial law. Just you wait, it'll happen in our lifetime. The bureaucracy can only grow like a cancer, and it doesn't matter who the president is—forgive me, Ronald Reagan," said Bernie.

"I've been thinking about going off-grid myself, Bern," said Ernie Fabrizi, a man I'd known from Christmas Eve gatherings at my great-uncle's house. "I have that cabin up in Cincinnatus, nothing as complex as your place."

"I'm telling you, it's a solid investment, Ernie," said Bernie. "Anyone can build a rain collection system, have a good stock of canned goods, proper protection. I'm not saying install a bunker like I have, but if you get yourself a place in the woods and don't have to rely on the electrical grid, you'll do alright."

I was nervous approaching the counter with my new gas mask filters. Bernie had said to always replace the filter when you got a new mask, but I didn't have enough to purchase it the week prior.

"Hey, Joey! Just these?" asked Bernie, inspecting the filters I'd set on his counter.

"Yes, sir. I'm just wondering if 40mm is the correct size?"

"Yeah, it'll fit perfect with that Israeli respirator you just got," said Bernie.

"What's up, kid? Planning a stink bomb attack at school?" said Ernie, grinning through yellowed teeth.

All the old men laughed as my face flushed in embarrassment.

"Nah, he's a prepper," said Bernie. "He knows his shit too, Ernie. I imagine you could learn a thing or two from him."

"Join the Navy, kid," said a Navy man whom I recognized, but had never caught the name of. "At sea you won't have to worry about gas attacks, or fallout."

"I think I might join the Army after high school," I offered.

The men erupted in laughter, slapping each other on the backs. Sure, they were mostly wearing Navy and Marine caps, but even the WWII Army vet thought it was amusing.

"Don't do it, kid," said Ernie. "Go to college—if you have the choice."

"You think they'll ever reinstate the draft?" asked the Navy man.

The guys began debating the merits of a professional military vs. conscription while Bernie rang me out. He placed a box of MREs on the counter.

"You can have these, Joey," said Bernie. "I haven't gotten as many Boy Scouts this winter. Do you know if they still teach cold-weather survival?"

"Oh, I don't know. I haven't been in the Scouts for a couple years now, due to sports. But thanks, Mr. Rogers," I said, grabbing the box and mask filters from the counter before heading out.

I now must admit that I omitted the various racial slurs for Japanese, Korean, and Vietnamese soldiers that littered the speech of the old men—and in turn some of the more interesting war anecdotes that I overheard that morning—not wanting to distract a more sensitive reader from the purpose of my narrative.

\#

To the great relief of my teachers, and hundreds of my traumatized peers, the hysteria that had overtaken Lestershire High had all but passed. I could tell that some of my classmates still weren't sleeping well, but at least they were again regularly attending class, and the general level of irritability and disorder in the school had returned to what would be considered acceptable for any confined space with 1,000 teenagers. The 'Nightmare Rock' had largely been pushed to the periphery of daily chatter, like an overplayed pop song from a prior season, or a flash-in-the-pan alt-rock band that had once been touted as the next Nirvana. The phenomena and lived experiences at the monolith had become so warped in their constant retelling, that the uninitiated could just as easily add their own flavor to the legend without having encountered the stone for themselves—often without a clue where the rock itself was located (I'd heard from Jeff Arnold in chemistry class that the stone glowed a greenish hue when you touched it.) While many had simply grown tired of the conversations aided by the stone's amnestic quality.

But I hadn't forgotten. I felt a suffocating anxiety over my disaster planning, that I wouldn't have enough done in time, over trying not to forget the images, and in attempting to piece everyone's visions together into a sensible, actionable narrative. I was in a lonely place now that my sister and friends had moved on, and I truly believed that I was the only one who knew something terrible was imminent. So, when I saw Stephanie Hoyt walk into Ms. Hall's math class one day—following a week's absence—looking as distraught as she had the last time I'd seen her, I couldn't help but reach out, if only for my own sanity.

I passed her a note, which she reluctantly accepted. It read: *Hey! I missed your math notes...and your actual math notes. I haven't been taking any. You been sick? Or just bad dreams?*

I watched Stephanie read my note and was pleased when she grinned. She wrote something and passed the paper back to me, and the conversation continued: *You do need my notes, don't you? :) But I really did have the flu or something. I've been having nightmares pretty often. They never really stopped since I touched that rock in the woods. I had one last night that was so intense!*

I felt bad for her, but also thrilled that she, too, recalled the stone as the source of her nightmares. Apparently, she'd never taken anyone out to the monolith, never passed on her mental anguish.

I wrote her back: *You never went back out to the rock with anyone? What happened in your dream?*

After Stephanie read my note, she took some time to consider her reply. I debated whether I should tell her about my MOPP suits and disaster prepping. She was the first crush I'd ever had. I didn't want her to die if I couldn't solve the puzzle and warn the right people in time. But I also knew that I might scare her off if I delved into my theories from the get-go; I had to take it easy with her.

Stephanie wrote: *I think I'm too much of a chicken to go back out there. Everyone else has stopped having bad dreams, so I hope mine will go away too. Anyway, in my dream I think I was at Poland Park, which is right by my house, and people were screaming and jumping into the river. They couldn't stop itching or something, and it was like they were peeling off their skin. It was so gross, and so scary.*

My own nightmares had been harrowing, to say the least, but it unsettled me to think that Stephanie had been plagued by the especially grotesque, and visceral, images of suffering.

I was able to pass her one last note before Ms. Hall caught on and told us to stop and pay attention. *Come over to my house later so we can make out... I'm kidding, I swear! Seriously, I want to show you what I've been working on, regarding the stone and all the bad dreams people have been having. We could even go back out there together. I think I might know a way to stop your nightmares.*

After class Stephanie met up with me in the hallway. "I think I can probably come over later, but I'll need a ride from my brother;" she said. "He's not exactly reliable...but we can definitely get together this weekend."

I couldn't believe that she was smiling now, and even seemed upbeat. I told her I'd see her later, then went off to my next class.

When I got home that afternoon, I laid out all my gear to show Stephanie. I really thought that, of all people, she might believe me, since she'd been having the nightmares for so long. If she came over; I knew there was a chance that I could lay out the evidence to her, that an apocalyptic event was imminent, and I'd finally have someone on my side.

I laid out my MOPP suits, put together my gas masks, brought out all my survivalist stuff I'd been hiding in my closets and under my bed. I had a few backpacks full of MREs, SpaghettiOs, various supplies to use once I got to a protected environment like a fallout shelter. I had collected a variety of gear and supplies in a relatively short time and my room looked more like a barracks than a teenage boy's bedroom.

"Joey, *what the hell* is all this?!" said Tim, who had stepped into my bedroom.

I spun around, surprised that he wasn't still napping. "Uh...I'm just getting ready for a camping trip with Jay and the Groome twins."

My dad dug around my equipment, picking out one of my gas masks for inspection. "You need six gas masks and potassium iodide tablets to go camping with the boys?"

I dropped the ruse. "These MOPP suits are gonna save us when the power plant melts down, Dad," I said, sheepishly.

"Christ, Joe. This has to stop!" I hadn't seen him this worked up in years. He was livid. A vein in his neck was even bulging. "You're obsessed with this crap. You've got to stop listening to that idiot Bernie—the highlight of that man's life was ten years working as a Navy cook—he knows nothing! I've spent twenty years as an engineer designing and maintaining some of the most complex systems in the world. There's not going to be a meltdown, the government isn't coming for our guns, and all you have to worry about is getting good grades and being a kid!"

"I really wish you'd believe me, Dad. There's this stone in the woods, and it was giving everyone visions of a disaster that would hit Lestershire, and I've been keeping a journal, and Mr. Verity says his family has a fallout shelter in Waverly..." I must've been babbling, because my dad just cut me off. To be fair, I knew that I'd sound crazy to anyone who hadn't touched the thrumming stone for themselves.

"That's enough! I want you to get rid of all this crap by the end of the week. You don't need a machete, or a dozen flashlights, or all these Army manuals. You're not going to grow up to become some agoraphobic Unabomber moron. Your sister's learning to drive; she's out with her friends, being a teenager. I always said I wouldn't say stuff like this to my own son, but you need to be interested in girls, sports, things that involve other people your age." He paused, as if to reconsider something he'd said. "Maybe you're gay. I don't care if you're gay—I'll love you all the same."

My dad then paced the room considering whether my recent behavior was just a symptom of a budding homosexuality.

"Okay, I'll get rid of it, Dad." I only said it to buy more time until I could figure out what to do. He seemed to relax a little once I relented.

"Thanks, pal. I appreciate it," he said. "I know it's hard being a teenager, but I'm only looking out for you." He then told me that he'd only come up to tell me that he got called in early to the power plant, and we said our goodbyes.

I was surprised when Jason appeared at my bedroom door, not an hour after my dad had gone.

"Hey, Jay," I said, feeling awkward as he inspected the gear I had all over the place. To be honest, I probably did go overboard in the volume of gear that I had acquired—certainly a case of quantity over quality.

"Hey, dude. I was wondering if you wanted to hang out. Maybe play video games or ride bikes."

"I can't go out. Stephanie Hoyt might come over," I said. "We can play video games if you want."

He smirked. "Stephanie Hoyt is coming *here?*"

"Yeah," I said, flatly. I wasn't in a jokey mood.

He picked up the machete and looked it over. "Joe, if Stephanie sees all this junk, she's going to think you're a serial killer..."

We both smiled. "Probably. But I doubt she can make it, anyway."

"What's your strategy if she does come over? Show her your doomsday stuff and get her to go off with you into the woods?"

"Jay, it's going to happen...soon," I said. I was practically pleading for him to remember. "I can show you; I've written everything down in my journal."

I went to my desk and pulled out my notes. "*Bright-green grass pushing through thawing sludge*," I read. "Stephanie's still having nightmares. She keeps dreaming of the river when it's high. Early spring makes the most sense."

"Is she really buying into all this?" he said, waving his hand at the MOPP suits and survival paraphernalia.

"I really don't get how you don't remember our plan to figure this thing out together," I said, raising my voice.

"Chill out. I'll go; no problem," said Jason, turning to leave.

I couldn't believe it. Jason had seen the valley burning. Our hometown mired in a cataclysmic event. We had talked about what we had seen, what our sisters had reported, for weeks. I couldn't bear the thought of him walking home some afternoon, or just coming out of his house, amidst the nuclear fallout, with nowhere to go. I knew exactly how I could make him remember. The stone would make *anyone* remember.

"Jay, don't go," I said. "I won't talk about this stuff, alright? Let's go out and play basketball."

His expression softened immediately. "Alright, cool. The park?"

"Yeah, let's go to the park. Maybe we can play a pickup game with some other guys."

I followed him downstairs, grabbed my sneakers. Lauren and Jenny were sitting at the kitchen table doing their nails.

"Where are *you two* going?" asked Jenny.

"To play basketball," I said, casually.

"Mom said we have to be home for dinner by 6," said Lauren to her brother. "I guess Dad's working late, but she claims she'll be home right at 6 with KFC, or something."

"We won't be gone that long," said Jason.

We rushed out the backdoor and found a basketball in the garage. It was only a five-minute walk to the court at Virginia Ave Park. There were two softball fields between us and the creek. As we shot around, I tried to think of a way I could convince Jason to come with me to the clearing. I knew if I could get him to cross the creek, he'd remember enough and would likely touch the stone out of a renewed curiosity.

"Ball's kind of flat," stated Jason. "I can't believe no one else is down here. It's almost warm out."

I agreed with him as I set up for a three in the corner.

"I can't stand it when it's not really cold but not exactly warm," said Jason. "I wish the summer would just get here so we can do more stuff outside."

"It's almost trout season," I offered as Jason hit a nice jumper from the top of the key.

"All the streams around here suck," he said. "My dad said he's going to take me fly fishing in the Catskills."

"Awesome," I said. "I heard some older guys talking about fishing Choconut Creek near here." I hoped it wasn't too obvious that I was leading the conversation.

Jason snorted. "Little Choconut? There's nothing but minnows and garbage back there."

I knew it would be a tough sell. We'd explored just about every inch of the surrounding neighborhoods on foot, bike, by skateboard. I didn't immediately reply but kept rebounding and passing the ball back to him.

"I guess we can go take a look," said Jason. "I've got to take a piss, anyway. It's probably better if I'm not within sight of the church."

"Yeah, good thinking," I said.

We walked between the two softball fields, then past one of the dugouts to get to the wide path leading down to the creek. It wasn't a five-minute trek.

"The creek's deeper than I remember," said Jason as he relieved himself in the stream.

"Snow melts in the spring, dude."

"Oh, yeah," said Jason, chuckling.

I walked out onto the creek, where some broken concrete slabs had been dumped. There were enough big rocks that I figured I could probably make it across without falling in. I hopped from stone to stone, finally slipping near the far bank, and soaking my right foot up to my ankle. The water still bore an icy chill from the waning winter.

"What are you doing?" asked Jason, staring at me dumbly from the other bank.

"C'mon, let's see if that weird stone's still out here."

"Huh?" He hesitated. "I don't want to get my new Jordans wet."

"They're not new, Jay. You wore them for all of basketball season—and to school."

He begrudgingly began crossing, stopping when he had gotten halfway.

"You have to use the stones now," I said.

Jason mumbled something, I assumed he was cursing me out. But he did continue, soaking his sneaker in the same vicinity as I had.

"*C'mon!*" he yelled, as he stumbled onto the soft bank.

I didn't say anything, just went into the woods, and he followed.

"I sorta remember us coming out here," said Jason. "It's weird. I can't remember whether it was two weeks ago or two *years* ago."

"It's just up ahead in this clearing," I said. The ground became rocky before we again emerged into the stony field of erratics. The monolith at the center seemed taller than I'd remembered. I didn't feel right being there, now that I knew what knowledge the stone was trying to impart. I honestly felt panicked at my first glimpse of it in months, and nearly turned and walked away—as if I could pretend that I'd never touched the stone...

Jason gasped. "Why don't I remember all these rocks, Joey?" His voice came out softer, weaker. "It's like I was never here; but I know we *were* here..."

As we approached the center, we had to step over heaps of litter strewn about the area. There were cigarette butts everywhere; even a few beer cans littered the ground around the base of the monolith. I was disgusted when I caught sight of some generic graffiti in the middle of the stone, obscuring a few of the petroglyphs: an anarchy symbol, a few initials, one of those S symbols that everyone drew in their notebooks. My classmates had certainly made their presence known; the stone now resembled a defaced bathroom stall.

Jason and I now stood side by side before the stone, inspecting the damage done by the spray paint. I paused when I thought I'd heard something—a humming that came out of nowhere. It seemed to have sprung into existence in *response* to my listening rather than the other way around. It was the same idling sound I'd heard months before, but this time it snuck up on me. It was like I was standing mere feet from the grill of a rumbling tractor-trailer. I swear I could feel the vibrations through the air.

"Do you hear that, Joey?" asked Jason.

"Yeah."

"I don't think we should touch it. I remember getting a headache, passing out..."

"We'll touch it together, Jay," I said, bracing myself. I was afraid, but it had to be done. "You'll remember everything..."

I grasped him by the elbow, as to guide him, and we both pressed our palms to the frigid rock. For a few seconds I felt the thrumming vibrato of the rock pass through my arm and into my chest, connecting me to whatever above or below gave the monolith its special purpose.

This time around I didn't feel myself fall into unconsciousness; there was no nausea either. I came to abruptly, Jason shaking me and repeatedly calling my name. I was on my side and my vision was momentarily blurred, but I was able to gradually focus on a few vibrant-green blades of grass that were emerging from the soft mud nearby.

"What happened?" I asked, as I rolled onto my back.

"When I woke up, I heard an explosion. It shook the entire hillside, Joey." His voice wavered.

"I didn't hear anything."

"You were out when I got up." I could see the fear and turmoil in his eyes. "I saw it again, Joey. I saw everything! The hillside burning, the valley covered in smoke right down to the river. We've got to go!"

I gathered my wits and Jason helped me to my feet. We raced out of the clearing and up the embankment. It would take too long to go back over the creek. We heard a few secondary explosions while we ran through the forest, and sirens were already blaring from down in the valley.

"Holy shit!" exclaimed Jason, now out of breath. He had been the first to reach the road, and moments later, I saw it too.

Above the tree line was a massive, billowing plume—what I could only surmise was the remainder of a mushroom cloud. Incidental smoke had arisen in its wake, and the air was quickly becoming tainted, acrid. Something big was now on fire.

Jason looked back at me, his face a ghastly pallor. "That looks like it's coming from the chemical plant!"

CANTICLE SIX

We never looked back nor did we utter a single word as we flew down the hill. By the time we reached my house, the sky had become an unsettling vision: a vast, gray canvas marred by monstrous, black clouds, illuminated by blazing, orange fires. Jenny and Lauren were out on the front lawn, watching the sky, captivated by the vivid, looming haze. I hadn't seen Jenny look so lost since the days following our mother's death.

Some of our neighbors had come out, or were at their windows, looking to the north, utterly confused, dumbfounded. I had become a spectator at that point, as I was also transfixed by the sights and sounds of the disaster. It was like the whole neighborhood was under some sort of group trance.

It was only when a fire truck tore up the road, blaring its siren, that I was shaken from my temporary paralysis.

"It's the chemical plant!" I shouted. My friends just looked at me dumbly. Of course it was. "We have to go up to my room and get the protective suits on, now!"

My friends followed me up to my room, but only because they were willing to be herded like sheep.

"No, don't put the gas mask on yet, Jay!"

Jason, Lauren, and I hurried to get our MOPP suits on, while Jenny stood by watching us. "Jenny, get the suit on!"

"What about Dad?" she asked.

"He wasn't at the chemical plant. He's across the river," I said. "Dangerous gases are about to settle into the valley. You need to get dressed in the chem suit, now!"

Lauren began crying and had stopped getting dressed.

"How do you know?" asked Jenny. Inside my room, away from the hectic scene taking place outside, she'd had time to think.

I didn't have time to delve into my research, to explain how I determined that the stone had allowed us glimpses into the future, to this very event. "What would cause and explosion like that on this hillside, Jenny? Just trust me for once. We need to get these suits on and get out of here!"

"What are you doing, Lauren?" asked Jason. He was already getting his boots on.

"*Mom and Dad were working today!*" she screeched in response.

I looked to Jason, who had stopped getting ready. It must've only hit him then that his parents were caught up in the worst of it.

"Really, what are these dumb jumpsuits going to do for us?" asked Jenny, who had gone over to comfort her friend.

"Stop it! Clouds of chlorine and fluorine gases are about to start drifting down the hill from the chemical plant. Shut your mouth and get your suits on, and don't forget gloves! I'll show you how to put your masks on after."

Jason encouraged the girls to get dressed and they obliged. Everyone was petrified. I did my best to help them with their suits, but I was a novice myself. I didn't know if everything was tied right; I just figured you didn't want any skin exposed, so I used duct tape liberally on wrists and ankles. I'd only really practiced with the gas masks. I didn't have proper training.

"Let's go!" I shouted, as if I were leading a platoon.

I thought about Stephanie as we ran down to the kitchen. If she had come over, I would've had a mask for her. I wondered if Bernie Rogers would make it to his bunker in time.

"Use the straps. It has to be really tight all around your face," I said, donning my mask. "Cup your hand over the vent here and blow out. Hand over the filter here, then breathe in. It should feel like your face is getting sucked in."

We were standing around, getting used to breathing through our masks. My friends looked alien to me in their disaster garb; sterile, inhuman. The masks concealed most of their faces, but I could see the abject terror in their eyes—a sliver of their humanity.

"Everyone good? No leaks? If not, tighten your straps some more," I said.

I wasn't sure what the next step was. I'd never really had a clear evacuation plan. I kind of figured my dad would be with us and he'd drive us down the highway.

I looked around and just happened to catch sight of a set of keys on top of the refrigerator. My mom's old beater Chevy still sat in the back of the garage. Another possession of hers he'd never had the heart to get rid of.

I grabbed the keys. "Jenny, you think there's still gas in Mom's car?"

"Huh?" she asked. She must not have heard me; our voices were muffled through the masks.

"Mom's car is in the garage. Here are the keys!" I shouted, holding them up.

"Who's going to drive?"

"You are!"

"I don't have my license!" she cried.

"You're the only one who has any driving experience," interjected Jason.

Lauren didn't add anything. She was whimpering beneath her mask.

I held the keys out to my sister. She reluctantly grabbed them, then we went out to the garage.

The sky was still dark, hazy. I wasn't sure if there were any chemicals in the air. I'd always read that you'd feel your skin tingling first. Our necks weren't fully covered. Jenny unlocked the car and we all piled in. Lauren and Jason sat in the back.

Rawr-rawr-rawr-rawr-rawr-rawr. Jenny held the ignition, but the car refused to start.

"Well, at least the battery isn't dead," said Jason.

"There's probably no gas left in the tank," said Jenny, before turning the key again. "Or maybe the car's just been sitting too long."

This time the car sputtered, turning over briefly before dying.

"I used to see Dad stomp the gas when he couldn't get his Charger to start," I said.

She stomped down on the pedal.

"No, I mean, you turn the ignition while pushing down on the gas pedal," I added.

She obliged and it miraculously worked! The engine roared to life as she held the gas down.

"Awesome, let's go!" shouted Jason, now leaning over the seat.

But Jenny just sat there.

"C'mon, what are you waiting for?" I said.

"I've never gone in reverse, Joey," said Jenny.

"Christ, it can't be that different than going forward," said Jason. "The sky's turning red. We've gotta get out of here."

My sister slowly pulled the gear stick back to R, then gradually released the brake. Miraculously, we made it out of the garage before she hit the driveway curb. Our driveway was three or four feet above our neighbor's yard.

"You have to straighten out!" I shouted. If a wheel went over the curb, I knew we'd be stuck.

"I didn't want to hit the house!" she shouted back at me. She'd at least had the sense to hold the brake once the wheel bounced off the curb.

"Turn the wheel to the left," said Jason.

It was slow going, but we eventually made it out of the driveway and into the street.

"Where am I going?" asked Jenny.

"Take a right on Memorial; we need to get on the highway," I said, thinking of Mr. Verity's bunker in Waverly. I knew it didn't make an ounce of sense to try and find this boarded-up shelter in a town I'd never been to—that we probably just had to get out of Lestershire to be safe—but it was the only plan I'd ever had, and I was too distressed to think of a better option.

Memorial Drive was eerily empty. We drove past Valleyview Cemetery—the sky above was enveloped in an amber hue. I could still hear sirens off in the distance, but it wasn't until we approached the main intersection in town that we started to see the bodies. A couple slumped over in the walkway near the Broadview Diner, a man lying face down on the sidewalk near a bus stop. Nobody remarked about the bodies, though I knew everyone must've seen them. The only corpse I'd ever seen was Mom's, and she'd lain peacefully in a silk-laden casket.

"There's a traffic jam up ahead," said Jenny. "I don't think I'll be able to get to the on-ramp to the highway."

"If we can't get to the highway, we'll just go around to Elmdale," I said, unsure of how we'd get around the traffic jam.

We approached the mess of stopped vehicles, where it was clear a panic had broken out. Cars were mashed together; shattered glass littered the road. There was no rhyme or reason to where people had stopped or lined up. As we weaved through the wreckage, we could see drivers slumped over their steering wheels; some were still gasping, choking on whatever toxic chemicals had permeated the air around us.

"Just drive on the sidewalk," said Jason, when it was clear we could make no more headway on the road itself.

Up ahead I could see a few bodies still writhing on the sidewalk, clinging to life by a thread. Jenny was able to drive in the grass to get around them, thankfully.

"This can't be good," said Jason. There was an orange fog up ahead.

"Do I drive through it?" asked Jenny.

"We can't turn around," I replied. "We're almost to the mall."

As soon as we entered the fog, I could feel my scalp begin to tingle.

"*Ahh, my neck's on fire!*" shouted Lauren.

I looked to my sister; I could see that her eyes were watering. "Keep going, Jenny!"

I felt tiny pinpricks on the back of my neck. I could only hope that this orange fog would dissipate as each one of us complained, even howled, about stinging skin or eyes.

"There's nowhere to go," said Jenny. We'd reached the stone wall at the edge of the Elmdale Mall property; there were still cars to our right and left.

"We'll have to get out and keep going," I said.

"I'm not getting out!" shouted Lauren.

"The fog isn't as bad, but we can't just sit here in it," I said.

Jenny, Jason, and I had already opened our doors and were getting out. Lauren stayed put. "No!"

Jason reached into the car and yanked his sister out. I helped him move her forward through the deadly haze.

"I can't really see that well," said Jenny.

I inspected her mask. She must not have had that great of a seal, because her eyes were red. "We'll get through," I said, grabbing her by the hand.

The four of us stumbled over the berm to the mall parking lot. We could see down to the roadway; there were a few people crawling along the blacktop, exposed to whatever chemical horrors had been unleashed on our town. No one could really scream or call out for help because they were choking on saliva and blood.

Lauren shrieked as we walked beside a parked Volvo. I recoiled when I saw the putrid face of a woman pressed against the driver-side window. Her skin had come off like some sort of cheese-like substance as it smeared across the glass.

"What the hell is happening?" asked Jason, to no one in particular.

Once we got to the western end of the mall lot we went back down to the road. Up ahead I could make out an orderly roadblock, made up of mostly camouflaged National Guard trucks and Humvees.

Jason hesitated when he saw it. "Why is there a roadblock? Why aren't they helping these people?"

I felt sick to my stomach. I knew what he was getting at. "We can't turn around."

Jenny was choking now. I could feel her growing weak as I put my arm around her to keep her upright and moving.

"What if they shoot us?" said Lauren.

Jason was practically dragging her by the arm now. "It doesn't matter. We don't have anywhere to go."

From a distance I couldn't make out any movement at the blockade, so I thought that it might be abandoned. I wasn't exactly relieved when the doors of the lead Humvee opened, and two serious-looking soldiers stepped out with their rifles at low-ready.

We kept going, and four more soldiers exited the vehicles, all in full, state-of-the-art MOPP gear. One of them yelled "Stop!" and then they surrounded us at twenty yards as we halted, raising our hands in the air. Jenny slumped against me, Jason and Lauren looked to me. I was terrified that we'd just be gunned down, and I even braced for a torrent of gunfire.

One of the soldiers quickly approached, his gun now lowered, and beckoned to me. "Let's go, let's go! We'll get you out of here!" I couldn't believe it. They were helping us!

Jason and Lauren stepped forward while I held my position, supporting my sister.

"Does she need assistance?" asked the soldier.

Déjà vu. Two of his comrades rushed in to help Jenny.

In seconds we were guided into the back of a large truck. They gave Jenny a mask with an attached oxygen tank, while a medic named Pacheco inspected us and asked us how we felt, what symptoms we were having. I was relieved when the truck started moving.

"You guys are lucky you had this equipment," said Pacheco, clearly surprised that a group of kids had secured and were operating in such gear. "Exposure to this mix of gases is absolutely lethal."

"Where are we going?" asked Lauren.

"Out west to Waverly-Sayre. It's the nearest medical center that isn't at risk of exposure," he replied. "We're having a hell of a time evacuating Memorial Hospital."

"What's with the blockade and guns?" asked Jason.

"We still don't know whether this was an accident or a terrorist attack," said Pacheco. "I don't think you kids really know how lucky you are, to make it out of this valley alive today."

"Yeah, lucky..." said Jason, looking to me. I thought he might've winked, but it was tough to tell through his mask.

CODA

I've had ample time to consider the events that took place that season. I'm about to start my second year at NYU. I've matured some in the intervening years; losing friends, teachers, and family members will do that. I've tried to keep my distance from my hometown, living and working in Manhattan since I graduated high school.

The northside of Lestershire is practically a ghost town now. The hillside beneath the plant has been all but razed, including most of my old neighborhood—no one sleds or plays softball at Virginia Ave Park anymore. Nearly half the town left after the calamity, which makes sense since most of them were employed or connected in some way to the now-bankrupt E. Johnson Chemical Corp. A total of 606 people died that terrible day, including Jason and Lauren's parents. My dad is alive, thankfully, but he's suffered from bouts of severe depression since the catastrophe. He feels like he let down his colleagues at the chemical plant, that he shouldn't have let himself get stretched so thin between his two jobs.

We moved south of the Susquehanna River during the cleanup, while Jason and Lauren relocated to Cortland to live with their grandparents. Jenny and I eventually lost touch with them. We kept our distance from our old neighborhood, and I've only returned to the monolith in the woods recently.

The thrumming stone is inactive now. I'm sure of it. The petroglyphs have all but faded and the rock is practically covered in graffiti. I inspected it up close, touched it, tried to glean any last bit of information it might have. I'm trying to connect my past to my present.

I've taken up anthropology at school, concentrating on the history and peoples of New York. I think I've discovered some Iroquois stories and songs which refer to seeing stones, and I've been trying to give them geographical locations. It's been difficult, but I'm positive there are more of them out there. In fact, I believe I've located one in the heart of Central Park just this past summer.

I still have nightmares about unpreventable catastrophes, but I really don't know whether they're at all connected to the stone. Is it possible that there is some sort of lingering precognitive power lying dormant in my synapses, leftover from my brushes with the stone in Lestershire? Perhaps. But I certainly didn't foresee the disaster that is George W. Bush becoming president! Nightmares tend to reflect the anxieties of your surroundings, so it's been easy conjuring new, and reliving old, fears in this massive, towering city.

I've written this memoir to make a record of, and to fully explore, my season in hell. In doing so, I hope to put this dreadful chapter of my life behind me. Over the last few months I've debated whether I have it in me to be a watchman again. I was practically useless in a town of 5,000. There are 1.5 million people in Manhattan alone.

Jenny's supposed to visit this week. I won't let her be a conduit again, but she might have some good advice. She's matured herself, and she's really the only other person I could tell. In fact, she's told me that she now remembers everything that happened—all the way back to our first contact with the stone—and not only that—she claims her short-term memory has become incredible, savant-like, even.

Joe Sullivan
Sept. 2, 2001

Summer Release Preview

The following is a featured story from the upcoming Cemetery Gates Media anthology *Other Voices, Other Tombs*. This collection will showcase original works from some of the finest horror authors of today.

"Three lanes deep" comes from the fiendishly talented mind of Gemma Amor, author of the well-reviewed, and hand-illustrated collection *Cruel Works of Nature: 11 Illustrated Horror Novellas*. Gemma has two forthcoming books: a novel *White Pines* (a paranormal mystery novel about an entire town that vanishes) and *Till the Score is Paid*, a collection of short stories, to be published by Giles Press in December. Gemma is also a frequent contributor to the popular *NoSleep Podcast*, *Shadows at the Door*, and she writes, produces, and acts in two of her own podcasts: *Whisper Ridge*, and *Calling Darkness*, which stars TV and film actress Kate Siegel.

Other Voices, Other Tombs. Edited by Brhel & Sullivan. To be released in Summer 2019.

Three lanes deep
by Gemma Amor

L ucy is stuck.

As traffic jams go, it is the worst she has ever encountered. Hundreds of cars stand gridlocked, nose-to-tail and three lanes deep on the motorway all around her. A broiling midsummer sun beats down mercilessly upon them all, and the air shimmers with a thick, soupy heat. It bounces off countless bonnets and windscreens, and she can see it rippling over the grey, worn tarmac, like wrinkles in a pond when a stone is thrown.

She has been trapped like this for almost an hour, now: trapped, desperately hot, and horribly miserable. There is no shade, no breeze, and no cloud cover in the sky. Just a blazing white ball of fire, burning relentlessly. Her car ticks and groans gently as the brutal heat forces the metal to expand, warp, contract again, an unwelcome percussive accompaniment to her misery. Her brother Lucas shifts in his seat beside her, a steady trickle of sweat making its way down the right side of his face. He keeps wiping it away with the palms of his hands, then shaking them to flick the sweat off. Little salty droplets splat onto the dashboard and across Lucy's right arm, making her flinch. It is driving her *mad*.

'Stop doing that, it's disgusting!' she snaps, wiping her arm with the bottom of her damp shirt in disgust.

Lucas lets out a frustrated moan, ignoring her and wiping his brow for the thousandth time.

'*Arrggghhh!*' he says, banging the steering wheel with his hands, letting his frustration and discomfort show. It takes a lot for his usually cool and collected exterior to slip, and Lucy can see that he is on the verge of losing his temper. He isn't the only one.

'It's hotter than the devil's arse crack in here!' he continues, his face turning an even brighter shade of red than it had been a moment ago. Lucy wonders briefly about spontaneous combustion, and how hot a person has to be before they actually melt, or burst into flames, or simply crumble and disintegrate into a pile of ash.

'Here,' she replies, listless, passing him an almost empty bottle of water. He takes it and swigs, then grimaces.

'Hot,' he says, passing the bottle back. 'Gross.'

The air conditioning in the car is broken and has been for well over a year. The siblings have been nagging their Dad to get it fixed, but he keeps muttering about the cost of parts and labor being more than the worth of the whole car, and so here they are, immobilized, the windows wound down as far as they will go, zombies sitting in a heat that is as thick as freshly poured tarmac. It pins them to their seats. Lucy feels as if a huge, hot cow is lying on top of her. She can't think properly. She can't speak. She can barely breathe.

'How much longer do we have to sit here?' She moans under her breath, beginning to feel woozy, and faint.

Her brother snorts.

'Well, if the fucking radio worked in this pile of shit car, we'd be able to get traffic updates, wouldn't we? But it doesn't work, does it. Just like the air con. And the windscreen wipers. And the front left indicator. And the satnav. Because Dad doesn't believe in fixing things, does he? Prick.'

They sit in silence for a while longer, before Lucy thinks to look at her phone. Her fingers, slick with moisture, slide uselessly across a blank, black screen.

'Phone battery's dead. Yours?'

Lucas shakes his head. 'Died about three hours ago.'

They sigh for the thousandth time and return to staring listlessly through the front windscreen.

Time passes.

A strange, rich smell slowly begins to permeate the air around them, faint at first, and then, as the minutes crawl past, with more intensity. Lucy wrinkles her nose. 'What's that?' she says, irritably, the glands in her mouth working overtime to produce saliva and fight back a sudden nausea. 'It fucking *stinks*.'

Lucas shifts in his chair, wincing. 'Christ knows. Probably some roadkill nearby, or maybe the tarmac melting. It *does* fucking stink.'

'I don't think it's tarmac.'

Lucas sighs. 'Well, I don't fucking know, Lucy, alright? You're welcome to get out and explore for me, if it bothers you that much.' There is something odd in his eyes as he says this, something...knowing. His words sound rehearsed, almost, stagey... disingenuous. Lucy cannot for the life of her figure out why, but she feels somehow as if Lucas knows where the smell is coming from and doesn't want to tell her.

They lapse into silence, and the smell intensifies. Lucy dismisses her doubts about Lucas as extreme fatigue on her behalf, and returns to staring out of the window, acutely aware that every moment that passes is a moment of her life that she will never recover, never enjoy. The futility of her situation depresses her almost to the point of coma, and her chin drifts towards her chest as she begins to doze.

The sun blazes on.

A sound swells in the distance. Lucy frowns, waking from her half-sleep. It sounds like a motor, but everything around her is now parked, handbrakes on, engines switched off. She twists in her seat, the leather sticking to her skin and tugging at it painfully. She manages to crane her head around and is just about to stick it out of her window for a better look, when a motorbike appears right next to the car, roaring past at a gleeful, breakneck speed, with mere millimeters to spare. Lucy has a split second to react, yanking her head backwards before the bike takes it clean off.

'Hey!' She shouts, shaking her fist after the bike like an angry old man in a cartoon. The motorbike and its leather-clad rider ignore her, weaving easily between the lanes of parked cars, vans, lorries and trucks, then disappearing from view.

She catches the eyes of three lads who are in the car immediately to the left of her, on the passenger side, her side. The driver grins at her, leans out of his own window, and shouts after the motorbike:

'*Wanker!*'

He makes the appropriate hand gesture to accompany this expletive. Lucy smiles back weakly, her heart thudding in her chest from shock, and then slumps back into her seat.

'There's always one, isn't there,' her brother says bitterly as the bike speeds off into the distance. 'Always one smug bastard who thinks he is better than us because he has two wheels instead of four.'

Lucy doesn't answer. She wishes she was on that bike, moving forward, only moving forward, making headway instead of baking in the midday sun in the middle of the fucking M4 like a tray of overdone flapjacks. And that smell, oh, *God*. That smell is worse now than ever before. She begins to think that Lucas is right about roadkill. It smells foul and yet sweet, like the sugar beet factories used to smell near her house, when she was a child. A headache pokes at her temples.

Another ten minutes creaks by.

The sun shines down. The temperature on the dashboard indicator ticks up another degree.

Lucy loses her battle with frustration. 'What the fuck *is* going on up there?!' she erupts eventually, gesturing vaguely at the long queue of stationary traffic in front of them. She is beginning to feel desperate. There is a new problem to add to her load: a burgeoning need to urinate has made itself known, despite, or perhaps because of, her dehydrated state.

Her brother shrugs. 'Probably a smash up ahead. I could see blue lights flashing earlier.'

'There are too many bloody people on this earth,' Lucy says, shifting in her seat to try and ease the pressure on her bladder.

Lucas sighs. 'You've said that quite a lot on this trip. You sound just like Dad, have I told you that?'

'Shut up, Lucas,' she replies, a silent, impotent fury building up inside her. Her bladder cramps, and she winces, and bites her lip.

Time crawls on, and nothing changes, except the smell, which gets worse, and worse, and worse, until she is convinced it is a living, writhing, tangible thing, invading her orifices, crawling down her throat, choking her. The smell, the cars, the heat, and the building pressure on her bladder: that's all her life has become, now. A collection of uncomfortable things to be borne. *I am going to live out the rest of my days in this traffic jam,* she laments to herself. *I will become a melted lump of a person, like the stub of an old candle left on a windowsill.*

The sun shines on.

The temperature readout on the dash clicks up to 33 degrees.

#

As the second hour of their predicament approaches, people begin to get out of their cars. They stretch luxuriously, and congregate in the gaps between lanes, standing around, smoking, crouching down; doing anything to avoid sitting and roasting in their tin boxes on wheels. It makes Lucy feel slightly better that there are obviously other motorists who haven't fixed their air-con, either. Doors open and shut all along the motorway, voices began to rise, and mingle, and gradually the feel of something almost festive spreads, as people united in their suffering do what they can to 'make the best of it'.

The lads in the car to the left of them get out, pop open the boot, pull out a cooler box of cold coke cans, and began passing them around. The driver of the car presses one into Lucy's hand through her open window.

'Here you go, sweetheart,' he says, smiling at her.

Can't he smell that? she thinks, swallowing back bile, but apparently, he can't. She smiles tremulously, grateful, now almost incapable of speech. The burning desire to go the toilet has grown all-consuming.

She looks at Lucas. 'I need to go to the bathroom,' she says, her voice small, and desperate. The smell is now so foul she fears she might faint. She can see it is affecting him too. The muscles in his jaw work overtime as he fights to control his stomach. A reluctant sympathy spreads across his face, nonetheless. 'Come on,' he says, opening the car door. 'I passed a woman in a camper van a ways back, before we got gridlocked. I bet she's stuck too, and I bet she'll have a toilet you can use, if we ask nicely.'

Lucy nods, on the verge of tears, and unpeels herself slowly from the sticky, hot leather of the car seat. Anything to get away from the cloying, all-pervasive stench of...whatever it was.

If she thinks it is hot in the car, she is in for a treat as she steps out onto the burning tarmac. It hits her like a bat to the face: solid, searing heat. She can feel it rising through the soles of her sandals. *Hell,* is all she can think, her bladder threatening to explode. *I'm in hell.*

The boys from the neighboring car are putting up a parasol they have somehow stashed in the boot of their car.

'Come and join us under here!' the driver says cheerfully as Lucy scans the motorway desperately, looking for the camper van Lucas mentioned.

'I've just got to...stretch my legs first,' she says, wild-eyed, searching for that blessed relief.

Her brother smirks, gives the lad a knowing look. 'Call of nature,' he explains in a conspiratorial tone, much to Lucy's mortification, and the boys chuckle as she turns beetroot red.

'Good luck with that!' laughs the driver, not unkindly, looking at the mass of cars and people all around. 'Not much privacy out here!' Lucy is silent, miserable, shifting from one foot to the other constantly.

'Come on, then,' Lucas says, and as an afterthought to the lads: 'Save us a spot under that brolly!'

'Will do!' says their new friend cheerfully, and the siblings turn and walk towards the camper van, which Lucy eventually spots parked about six cars back, in the slow lane. It seems to glow in the sunshine, the promise of relief a holy grail to her right now.

As they approach, Lucy hobbling and holding her stomach, she takes comfort in two things: that the smell is subsiding the further she gets from her car, and the fact that the van is more of a full-scale motorhome than a camper, a huge old chrome thing, an American-style Winnebago. It gleams like a great silver bullet in the glare of the sun, and is hard to look at, the closer she gets, so she must shield her eyes.

And the driver of the van is indeed a woman, as Lucas had said. She sits next to her vehicle in a folding camp chair, a cold glass of something in one hand, a small umbrella that she is using as a parasol held elegantly in the other. She wears huge black sunglasses and a massive sun hat that throws her whole face into shadow. She looks as if she is on holiday in the French riviera, not stuck in a traffic jam on a shitty motorway alongside thousands of other unfortunates.

Lucy lets her brother do the talking.

'Hi there,' says Lucas, his easy, friendly manner having returned to him.

The woman smiles and lifts an eyebrow above the rim of her glasses, an inquisitive and sexy gesture that Lucas appears to appreciate. By this point, Lucy couldn't care less if she has five pairs of eyes stuck to the ends of each fingertip, she needs to piss so badly. She is so close to losing control of her bladder that her whole body is now cramped with the effort of not letting go, not like this, not in front of rows and rows of people... *Just hang on*, she keeps thinking, over and over. *Just...hang...on!*

'Hello,' the woman says, in a deep, husky voice that makes Lucy think of cigarettes.

Lucas turns his charm up to ten on the dial.

'I don't suppose we could ask a *huge* favor, could we? We've been stuck in this traffic jam for almost two hours, now, and my sister here doesn't feel very well.

In fact, to tell the truth,' and here, Lucas lowers his voice in an attempt at saving Lucy's dignity, 'To tell the truth, she desperately needs to use the bathroom, but...well. Out here...there aren't even any trees she can hide behind. And we were wondering, as you have this big van, whether you might allow her to use your bathroom? If you have one? You'd be helping us out in desperate times.'

Lucy is *beyond* desperate now, hopping from foot to foot, tears welling in her eyes. She has seconds before she cannot hold it anymore.

'I'm so sorry to ask,' she says, her voice wobbling with strain. 'I mean, I'll pay you for the inconvenience...'

The woman holds up a hand to silence her.

'Don't be silly,' she says in that cool as a cucumber voice. 'I've been there, I understand. Of course, you can use my bathroom.'

She stands gracefully, folding the umbrella, and opens the side access door to the van. 'Just in there,' she says, pointing to a small wooden cabinet inside. She has an odd, secretive smile on her face, but Lucy doesn't have time to think about this. She only needs relief, and almost faints with gratitude as the woman holds the door open for her.

'Thankyou, thankyou, *thankyou*! You are my hero!' she says, almost sobbing, and dives inside without further hesitation.

Lucy scrabbles at the cabinet door, and then fumbles to shut it behind her. She sees a fully-flushable toilet mounted to the wall to the left of her. She hastily drags her clothes down past her knees, fingers and hands now ten sizes too big for her. She is sweaty, and hot, and everything is swollen, sticking and catching in the moisture of the day. She wrestles with her knickers and eventually, they do as they are told, and she finally,

finally, blissfully, *wonderfully* is able to relieve herself. Water jets out of her in an urgent, hot stream of relief. Afterwards, she sags against the small toilet cabinet door, panting, overcome. *Blessed, blessed relief,* she thinks, thanking her lucky stars for the Winnebago and the woman in dark glasses.

She flushes, and resumes the wrestling match with her sticky, sweaty clothes. Once dressed properly, she looks around for some soap. There is a dispenser on the far cabinet wall, mounted above a tiny chrome sink, and she reaches out to depress the pump.

Something moves just behind the dispenser.

A tiny, *tiny* movement, barely perceptible, but it catches her eye. Lucy freezes, arm outstretched.

The movement occurs once more. She squeaks in surprise, and then leans in closer, peering at the source.

And finds a hole, cut into the cabinet wall, very like an empty knot-hole that you find in wooden floorboards sometimes. It is perfectly round, and about the size of a coin.

And there is something alive behind it.

'What the fuck?' Lucy murmurs, all previous distress now forgotten as she stands stock-still in the tiny closet toilet.

Behind the wall, there is more movement. Another small noise. She frowns, and leans in closer, trying to see what is behind the hole. Is someone else in the van? A partner maybe, or a pet, in the next partition? Lucy had thought the woman was alone, she gave that impression, but she hadn't exactly paid too much attention, either way- she'd been distracted.

Another slight shifting, and another noise. A distinctly... *human* sounding noise.

Almost...a moan.

Moaning?

Lucy's brain immediately leaps to the worst possible conclusion.

Peeping Tom.

Pervert.

Spyhole.

Voyeur. Watching me, in the toilet.

No *wonder* that woman had been so keen to let her in! It's obviously something she does, some perverted kink she's into. Sure, you can use the facilities! But there's a price to pay: your privacy.

Oh God, Lucy thinks, *what if there are cameras rigged up?*

Suddenly angry, she thrusts her right eye close to the hole and peers in, trying to identify the source of the moaning.

And she sees a man in the half-dark, bound, gagged, and propped upright in a small adjoining storage cabinet.

#

A thin light leaks into the cabinet, probably from cracks around a door Lucy can't see, or more missing knotholes in the wood. The light sits gently upon the man's prone form like dust, highlighting his face and the bare skin of his shoulders, which move up and down in jerky, panicked twitches.

Lucy stares in disbelief at him, slowly registering the cable ties about his wrists and ankles, the lack of clothing except for stained and dirty underwear, the blood. He is *covered* in blood, as if painted with it, and his eyes are wide, nostrils flared with a mad type of terror. He moans again, and makes a gurgling noise, low in his throat. He knows someone is there. He wants Lucy to help him.

Oh, God. Oh, God, is all she can think. Her hand flutters up to her mouth. She is cold all over, an alien feeling given the heat of the day. Lucy jerks her head back from the hole, heart thumping, her own blood pounding in her ears. She checks behind her to see if the toilet door is still locked. It is.

Trembling, she slowly puts her eye to the peephole once more.

The man rolls his head back, the moaning, gurgling sound rattling out into the closed space. Then, Lucy sees the wound on his neck. Fresh, and deep, and wet, like a wide-open mouth. His throat has been cut, probably only moments before she'd walked into this van. He is dying.

Lucy recalls the odd, secretive smile on the mysterious woman's face as she'd opened the door for her, knowing what was hidden inside the van, thrilling to her own dirty little secret.

The man continues fight for his life, blood sheeting down his naked body. Paralyzed, with her face glued to the wall, Lucy watches as he struggles to breathe, his chest fluttering with tiny, futile movements as he tries to draw air in through his severed windpipe. His focus locks onto her one, disbelieving eye, peering in at him through the spy-hole, and he pleads silently for help, but she knows, deep down, in some instinctive way, that he is beyond help. And so, Lucy watches, a prisoner in time, a statue, and the man moans again, and then gargles and chokes, drowning in his own blood. Red mist sprays from his mouth and bubbles from his neck and finally, in a slow and graceless defeat, his chin sinks to his chest. He falls sideways, slumped, dead.

Dead.

The spell is broken.

Lucy starts to scream, and then bites down on her wrist, hard, to stop herself.

Out, she thinks, her body alive with adrenaline and fear. *I have to get out.* And then, because she loves him:

My brother is out there.

I can hear him, talking to...that woman...and I have to get him out, away from this, before she slits our throats, too!

But as Lucy opens the toilet cabinet door, slowly, softly, she understands that it is too late. She can hear voices, close to her, closer than they would be if they were both still standing outside the van.

She inches cautiously out of the toilet, trying to assume a neutral, pleasant expression, and failing. She remembers the eyes of the dying man in the closet, wide, glaring, begging for her help, then fixing on something far away as his life leaves him.

There is the unmistakable sound of a bottlecap being popped off a beer bottle, and then another, staccato, and a chink, glass upon glass. Then, laughter, both male and female. Lucy edges around the corner of the toilet cabinet, and sees her brother, inside the van, with the woman, an ice-cold bottle of Heineken on its way up to his mouth.

'Lucas!' she shouts, as the bottle grazes his lips.

'What?' he says, pausing momentarily, a guilty look on his face. 'Might as well make the most of it!' He chuckles, winking at the woman. Lucy feels sick, and powerless. She has no doubt that the beer is drugged, and that one solitary sip will be enough to put her brother out like a light. The woman has removed her sunglasses. She watches Lucy with bright, cold, intelligent eyes, assessing her like a bird assessing an insect.

'You can't drink and drive, Lucas,' Lucy says, feebly, avoiding the other woman's gaze, and knowing that the game is up. 'Besides, I don't feel well. I'd like you...I'd like you to walk me back to the car.' She tries to communicate that something is horribly wrong with her eyes, but the idiot only has eyes for the woman, who is, admittedly, gorgeous—Lucy can see that, now. She has long legs and long dark hair, and full, red lips. She's also a murderous predator, but Lucy guesses that doesn't translate so well, at first glance.

Lucas makes no move to depart, so Lucy lunges forward, grabbing his wrist.

'Come *on!*' she hisses, low and forceful, pulling him away, towards the door, towards safety, and the crazy woman puts down her beer bottle, in a slow, graceful, and deliberate movement, and reaches into a pocket for something hidden, and takes a step forward, and Lucy feels as if her heart will burst from fear, as she pulls and pulls urgently on Lucas' wrist, trying to drag him to safety, trying to leave the nightmare van, and the woman takes another step forward, and something bright, and shining slides free from her pocket, and Lucy can see that it is a knife, she can tell that Lucas hasn't spotted it yet, and she feels a scream swelling in her throat, and then...

And then, she hears it.

Or, more accurately, she becomes *aware* of it, despite everything else that is happening. It rises and looms, like an approaching wave. Quiet, at first, then building in intensity and urgency.

It is the sound of people, screaming.

#

Lucy rips her eyes away from the woman, reluctantly, trying to establish which threat is the greater threat, and glances to the open door to see what is happening outside. Because something...something is happening. Something somehow worse than the dying man in the

106

closet. All the hairs are up on the back of her neck, and her arms prickle with gooseflesh.

Something...*terrible* is going on.

There is a blur of activity, and a man races past, eyes wide with panic. His shirt is red with spray patterns of gore. Within moments, he is gone, running for his life, his arms and legs pumping hard. Lucy hears a *thump*, and a large, metallic screeching sort of crash in the distance.

'What the fuck?' she says, moving as if in a dream towards the door, towing Lucas behind her, for she has not let go of his wrist. The woman with the knife seems to have lost interest in them, and is frozen, like a deer in headlights, nostrils flaring as she listens to the oncoming tide of screams, crashes and thuds.

'What is it?' Lucas asks, his voice hollow.

Another streak of movement, and another man stumbles past, and then a woman, and then more people, children, men, women, old, young, dogs... Everyone is suddenly running, running and screaming, a desperate exodus of people abandoning their cars and racing away from...

From something.

But what? Lucy thinks, unable to make sense of what is happening. The screeching, crashing, squeezed metal noise gets closer, followed by loud, distinct thumps that shake the ground, rattling the walls of the Winnebago.

SCREECH! She hears, and then *CRUNCH!*

SMASH!

THUMP!

Hundreds of voices rise up in anguish, and panic, and Lucas and Lucy look at each other, wide-eyed.

'Let's go,' her brother whispers, his face white, and then they are out of the van, and running too, running for their lives, like small, feral animals fleeing a burning forest. The woman in the van, the body in the cabinet, it all pales in comparison to what is happening around them. The thumps and crashes get closer, and closer, and the ground shakes beneath the weight of something monstrously huge. Lucy trips, ploughing forward, her ankle turning under her, and is almost trampled underfoot by the crowds of people behind, but Lucas hauls her up just in time. She regains her footing, sobbing, almost blind with terror, limping on regardless, and realizes that they are moving in the wrong direction, because whatever it is behind them is herding them along like cattle, *towards* something. It hits her like a lightning strike that their only hope for survival is to break free of the tangled, scared stampede, and get off the motorway.

And so, Lucy makes an abrupt, ninety-degree turn, gripping her brother's wrist so hard she can feel her nails digging into his flesh, dragging him behind in her slipstream, and she crashes into men, and women, all these people, all of them running in the *wrong direction*! But she doesn't stop, doesn't look back. She smashes her hip into a car, bounces off, catches her outstretched arm on the open boot of another, keeps going. She is headed for the bank of the motorway, knowing that their best chance lies in getting off the tarmac, and away from the road altogether. The squealing, crashing noises move closer, and there is something else coming now, too, a smell not unlike the smell that leaked out of the boot of their car earlier that day as it sat stinking in the sun, not unlike the smell in the cabinet where the man with a slit throat lay drowning in his own blood, and Lucy knows what it is suddenly: it is the stench of death.

Death is coming for them, on huge, heavy feet.

Then Lucy, who is running and limping forward like a soldier through no-man's land, remembers something.

She remembers the body in the trunk of their car.

#

The edge of the motorway is closer now, and beyond the vehicles and crowds she can see a bright field of ripening wheat. It's dotted with vibrant red poppies. From here they look like drops of blood.

Lucy and Lucas make a final push through the charging throngs of people and throw themselves over a burning hot metal crash barrier that lines the edge of the motorway. This catapults them into a ditch, which they roll into, and then crawl out of, lurching onwards into the wheat field. Long, dry stalks, some of which are still green, brush against their legs as they move, whispering things to them. It is as if a thousand thin, sibilant voices are singing the same song, and the song is an ugly one:

We know what you did, the wheat stalks say. *We know.*

A great, spine-chilling roar lifts into the air around them like a flock of black starlings taking flight, swirling about, filling every available inch of space with unending rage and pain and torment. The siblings collapse to the ground, flattening the wheat stalks, clamping their hands over their ears, from which blood now trickles, as it does from their nostrils. The earth shakes with those colossal steps. Lucy can bear it no longer. She opens her eyes, and understands, at last, what is happening to her.

She is in hell.

Before her, rising above the wheat and the cars and the people like a vast monument to the dark, strides a horse-headed beast, a skeletal thing on corded legs, naked, soiled, and trailing thick banners of acrid smoke behind it. Those banners curl and climb into the blue sky, reaching for the sun. Massive, satin-black wings flex on the beast's back, creating a shuddering new horizon, throwing those who scuttle below it into the shadows.

It walks carefully, picking its way through the traffic jam, scanning the motorway, and then, at what seems at first to be on a random whim, it brings one vast, hoofed foot down, hard, upon a vehicle. The metallic, squealing noises make sense, now, as car after car, vans, including the Winnebago, lorries, bikes and trailers are trampled into thin masses of warped, smoking metal and glass. *But it isn't random, it is searching*, Lucy realizes, searching, with its empty eye-sockets, looking for something, choosing which cars to destroy, and which to save.

And then it stops. There is silence for a blissful second, where not even the wheat sings to them. Lucy holds her breath, as does Lucas. The beast stills, lifting its head high, scenting the air. It brays, flexing its wings once more, and then the vast, ancient, evil head swings slowly towards them.

There is no escape, Lucy thinks, and she closes her eyes as the ground shivers beneath her. She has set herself on this path, brought herself to this place, her and her brother, *thou shalt not kill,* it says in the Bible. They knew the rules, from birth, but chose to ignore them. They killed, they murdered, they committed the ultimate sin, and now they are here, alone in a field of wheat dotted with bright crimson poppies, and the very earth is shaking.

Lucy opens her eyes one last time, the smell of death stealing into her mouth, and comes face to face with the beast. It stares at her with empty holes for eyes, and if she looks hard enough, she can see fire, in the distance, and in the fire, the bodies of thousands of people who are all just like her, writhing in agony.

Then, it raises one leg, and Lucas is screaming beside her, but Lucy is tired, and doesn't want to run anymore.

The foot comes down.

The sun shines on.

And, in a parked car on an abandoned motorway in the middle of a steaming hot summer's day, blood drips from the trunk, running down the resin bumper, and pooling onto the tarmac.

It sizzles as it lands.

Fall Release Preview

The following is an original story from the third volume of our *At the Cemetery Gates* horror anthology series. To be released in October 2019.

The Wax Man Cometh

My husband Anthony was a beautiful man. At thirty, you'd still call him boyishly handsome, though he had the sort of strong jawline that you'd usually only see on sporting goods store mannequins. I often kidded with him, that he'd just need to grow some stubble (and age a few decades) to pass for a young Jon Hamm. He'd retort that he couldn't have facial hair because of his volunteer firefighter duties—the necessity of creating a tight seal between oxygen mask and skin—though we both knew that it would take him an eight-day week to grow a five o'clock shadow.

Anthony and I had always been a quirky couple. We both gravitated toward the strange and macabre in our choices of art and entertainment. We toured cemeteries, went on ghost walks, and chose lodging based on advertised hauntings. On our way to the Jersey Shore for our honeymoon, we took a full day to tour the Mütter Museum in Philadelphia, to see all the ghastly medical and anatomical oddities on display there.

When we began looking for our first house, we knew we weren't going to live in a typical ranch home in a typical neighborhood. We first sought out old churches, small chapels, and renovated funeral parlors, and almost purchased a former Methodist chapel on the banks of the Tioughnioga River. Before fate intervened in the form of a once-in-a-century spring flood, only days before we were supposed to close on the property. Anthony and I were relieved that we hadn't been underwater on a mortgage and with the property—though we were still disappointed, as we had grand ambitions for that little chapel and its working bronze church bell.

It was almost too perfect when a few months later, a former train station-turned-museum came up for sale. It was in our price range and only a town away from where we were renting at the time. Small towns in New York had been dissolving for years, villages that had been around since the 18th and early 19th centuries were fading away, and historical societies, like churches, were selling off properties at bargains. The purchase and our move into the mint green train station went smoothly.

There were quite a few pieces of furniture and general clutter leftover from the building's turn as a museum, and even from its time as a train station. Anthony loved the yellowed books and papers that he'd find tucked away in the beaten wooden furniture and 20th century filing cabinets. He read up on the history of the property at the library, which was only next door, and would often come home on a weekend afternoon with some new story or anecdote.

"'Binghamton was jarred at 9:45 o'clock on Saturday night and the western sky, for a moment, was aflame. Buildings trembled, people ran into the streets, and there was talk of an earthquake,'" said Anthony, reading aloud from a newspaper clipping he had found on microfiche, one Saturday morning.

"So, was it an alien invasion?" I joked, interrupting his flow.

"No, Sherry, two trains collided here in 1901, and one of them happened to be carrying dynamite!" he stated. "Listen to this: 'A flash as if the Heavens were on fire followed and before it had died away a

114

deafening roar which sent its vibrations for seventy-five miles announced that the ruin had been complete.'"

"Anyone die?" I asked, morbidly curious.

He nodded. "'The dying groaned as they writhed in awful pain on the ground in the fields nearby where they had been thrown by the explosion.'"

"That's intense..." I said. Anthony was grinning at me, not veiling his excitement in the slightest.

"This place has to be haunted," stated Anthony. "It sat abandoned for decades after the fire, and the historical society only brought more stuff in after the renovation. There's still so much here that I haven't gone through..."

"Anthony, I love the place—you know I do—but we're going to have to get a dumpster and start throwing out some of your 'historical' stuff," I said. "We're going to need space too."

It's burned into my memory, the way he smiled at me then. I still get weak in the knees thinking about it.

"Yes, there'll be space for everybody. We'll need room for a couple kids, a pack of dogs, maybe even a cat..." I stopped him from going on and on by kissing him.

It was a few weekends later that we got to the nuts and bolts of clearing out Anthony's 'historical stuff' from the basement. It was mostly broken furniture, filing cabinets full of the day to day operations of the museum, and cardboard boxes full of junk. But what I had my eye on—and what I had wanted to toss out since the first time I stepped foot into that basement—was a life-size wax figure of a train conductor.

"Tony, please tell me that Mr. Conductor can go today?" He furrowed his brow, which was his way of letting me know that he'd at least consider it.

"Tony, he's all droopy," I pleaded. "We couldn't display him anywhere like that. People would think we're shabby—and he's creepy."

I was right. The blue suited, elderly conductor had been through one too many hot summers tucked away down there. He was already partially melted; his face mimed the worst of the stroke patients I'd seen at the hospital where I worked.

Anthony went over to the wax figure to inspect him up close. After a few quiet moments, he placed his hand on the man's shoulder and turned to me. "Yeah, he is pretty creepy looking. But he is a conductor, and this was a train station..."

I was genuinely irritated, that my husband didn't immediately agree to toss the damaged wax man out. "Please, Anthony, he's got to go. I don't know that he won't star in my nightmares. Just look at him."

Anthony put his arms around the conductor and tried to lift him. "Christ. This thing's heavier than I thought it would be."

"Well, don't strain yourself, Tony," I said. "We'll get a dolly or something and then get him out of here."

"Sure thing, babe."

Over the next couple weeks, I thought little of our conductor in the basement. I knew eventually Anthony would get rid of it—if only to please me—and he and I were busy with work and decorating the main living areas of the house, anyway. I was exceedingly happy with how things were going at the time. We were even talking about a timeline for us getting pregnant.

When I came home from work one Friday evening with a bag of groceries, I parked in the little lot next to my quaint, green train station. I thought it was strange that Anthony's car was gone. He was always home before me and he rarely went out without sending a courtesy

116

text. As I unlocked the kitchen door, I considered that maybe he'd gone out on a call for the fire department. He'd recently been promoted to deputy fire chief at the engine company and had recommitted himself to responding to every call.

As soon as I opened the door and stepped foot into the house—before I could even turn the light on—I spotted a man standing in the kitchen! I dropped my groceries and flipped the light on, ready to defend myself... I clutched my chest and released a ragged sigh, when I realized it was only the wax form of the train conductor. It took me a few moments to gather myself, and I grimaced at the egg yolk that was seeping out of the bag and onto the hardwood floor. I couldn't believe that Anthony had done that to me, and I was livid when he came through the door a few minutes later.

"That wasn't funny, Tony! I practically had a stroke when I saw that thing in here!"

Anthony paused in the doorway—a pizza box in hand—unsure whether he should make a run for it. "Oh, the conductor... Sorry, babe. I got him upstairs, but then I wasn't sure what to do with him. I don't think we can just put him out to the curb for garbage pickup."

I huffed at him, still shaken from my encounter.

"I got pizza!" He grinned dopily, which caused me to lose most of my head of steam.

"The wax man has to go!" I pouted. "He looks even more disfigured in the light up here."

"I'll take care of it in the morning—I swear."

We settled in for the night watching Netflix— eating in the living room at my suggestion—I thought I'd get sick to my stomach if I had to dine within view of our melted-cheese-faced housemate.

It was around five the next morning when Anthony got called to a fire. He scrambled out of bed and we barely exchanged 'I love yous' before I was back to sleep. When I awoke at seven, and padded downstairs, I didn't immediately notice that the conductor was missing from the kitchen. I made coffee and was headed toward the living room, when I was once again startled by the sight of the wax man. The conductor was now in the rear hallway, facing me, and positioned as if he were guarding the rear door.

"Shit!" I burned my hand when some of my scalding coffee spilled out. I rushed to the kitchen and ran cold water over my injury. I didn't care why Anthony had taken the time that morning to move the wax man into the hallway. I was determined to finally get the damned thing out of my house.

I couldn't get around the conductor to get to the back door, so I tried pushing him in order to get by—but he was too heavy. After some time struggling, trying to make any type of headway, I thought of a much easier route.

I went outside and grabbed a length of rope from the shed and went up the back stoop. The door opened out, so I figured all I had to do was secure the rope around the conductor's torso and give him a good pull to get him to topple down the back steps. When I had the wax man tied, I heaved on the rope and was surprised when he came tumbling down with minimal effort! I had to jump out of the way as he broke into a myriad of pieces on the stairs. I laughed at his clean decapitation—his warped face staring up at me, a bizarre mix of placidity and agony—and even kicked his deformed head across the grass.

I then considered how I could dispose of him. We didn't have unlimited garbage removal, so I knew he wouldn't all fit in the trash bin the following week.

"You're wax. You can burn!" I stated, gleefully, when I remembered that we kept a gas can in the shed for the lawnmower.

I used a snow shovel to pile up the broken pieces of our train conductor on the nearby blacktop, then doused him in gas and set him on fire. I watched him become engulfed in intense flames and he soon eerily melted away into a thick pool of blue and white—the pool itself burned for some time, and I watched it in a trance-like state, satisfied with what I had done.

After the fire finally extinguished itself, I let the wax puddle cool, and as I was considering what I'd now do with the tar-like globs—which I knew I'd have to scrape off the parking area—my cell phone rang.

"Hello?"

"Sherry. This is Ronnie," came the familiar voice. Ronnie was Anthony's fire chief. "Anthony's been hurt and he's on his way to the hospital. Do you want me to send someone to pick you up?"

I began to panic. My whole body went limp and I really didn't know if I could drive to the hospital. "Memorial?"

"Yes. He should already be there," said Ronnie.

"Is it bad, Ron?"

"It's bad, Sherry. I'm sorry."

"I'll be there sh- shortly," I stammered.

I raced to the hospital. I was furious when they didn't let me go and see him right away. Ronnie tried to console me, but I was a mess, as anyone in my situation would be. All the guys from the firehouse were there. They all looked rough. An abandoned furniture factory had caught on fire, and it has been one hell of a morning for every firefighter in the county.

A nurse named Gloria came out periodically to give me brief updates. I worked in medical billing, so I didn't really understand the technical things she was telling me. I was relieved when she finally said I could go up his room in the intensive care unit to see him.

"Mrs. Kearns, your husband is stable, but he is in critical condition," said Nurse Gloria. "His physician will likely advise that we fly him to Syracuse's burn unit."

For all the talk in the waiting room about the fire, no one had let slip the extent of Anthony's injuries. I was sweating profusely even before we entered the hot hallways of the ICU.

"What percentage of his body is damaged and to what degree?" I did know the magic numbers of survivability, being a firefighter's wife. I was hoping for second degree burns, less than 50% of his body, some serious lung issues due to smoke inhalation...

"Right now, we're estimating that 60% of his body has received third-degree burns."

I collapsed against the wall as we walked. Gloria steadied me and took me down the hall to his room.

Anthony was being attended to by two nurses in the small room. They were giving him shots, running multiple IVs, I can't remember the details—I was strangely ecstatic, giddy even, when I saw his beautiful, unmarred face.

"Anthony?" I said it softly; I didn't dare touch him. He opened his eyes. He couldn't talk, the machines were breathing for him. He was covered in bandages. We made eye contact. It was enough at the time. He was aware of me.

Anthony remained stable for the next twenty-four hours. The doctors were planning on airlifting him to a major hospital an hour away in Syracuse. I thought that he had a fighting chance. I hadn't left the hospital. I'd just gone to get a coffee. When I returned, I saw that he had yanked the tubes out of his throat. He was gasping for air.

120

I reached to hit the emergency button to call the nurse, but his bandaged hand grasped mine before I could.

"I... love... you... Sherry." His voice was barely a whisper. I leaned in and told him that I loved him, that we needed to get his tubes back in.

He nearly sat himself up. I gently nudged him back to the bed. "What is it? You have to take it easy, Tony. I can't believe you..."

"I tried to get to you. I couldn't get through," he wheezed.

"What are you trying to say, Tony?" I leaned in closer, staring into those endless green eyes of his. There was terror there. Fear of the unknown.

"Sherry!" he gasped. *"I saw you...in the fire!"* He began coughing horribly, it was only moments before Gloria and another nurse rushed in to put his tubes back in.

Soon after, Anthony had closed his eyes for the last time. He passed away early in the morning while I slept soundly in a chair by his side. I didn't want to stick around the hospital after that. I shook off the grief counselor, held in my tears, signed what I needed to sign so they'd let me go home. I just wanted to be in our bed, hug his pillow and smell him—then maybe I could cry for a couple days.

But when I returned home, I was astonished to discover that he was there waiting for me. No, not the conductor; he was still a hardened, waxen smear on the pavement outside. Standing in the back hallway, in full firefighter kit, was my beautiful Anthony—a pristine wax replica, every intimate detail down to the mole behind his right ear.